Edwin Abbott

A Second Latin Book

SALZWASSER
VERLAG

Edwin Abbott

A Second Latin Book

Reprint of the original.

1st Edition 2023 | ISBN: 978-3-37514-376-3

Verlag (Publisher): Salzwasser Verlag GmbH, Zeilweg 44, 60439 Frankfurt, Deutschland
Vertretungsberechtigt (Authorized to represent): E. Roepke, Zeilweg 44, 60439 Frankfurt, Deutschland
Druck (Print): Books on Demand GmbH, In de Tarpen 42, 22848 Norderstedt, Deutschland

A

SECOND LATIN BOOK.

CONTAINING THE RULES OF SYNTAX WITH ILLUSTRATIONS,
EXAMPLES FOR CONSTRUING,

AND

CÆSAR'S ACCOUNT OF HIS TWO INVASIONS OF BRITAIN,

WITH

EXPLANATORY NOTES AND A VOCABULARY.

BY

EDWIN ABBOTT,

HEAD MASTER OF THE PHILOLOGICAL SCHOOL.

———•———

LONDON:
LONGMAN, BROWN, GREEN, LONGMANS, & ROBERTS.
1858.

PREFACE.

THIS book is intended to contain, in a cheap and concise form, so much of the Latin Syntax as will enable a beginner to parse accurately and construe upon sound principles.

It assumes a thorough knowledge of the Accidence. Long experience has convinced me that the grammatical inflexions of a language are only firmly impressed on the memory when learned "by rote," without trusting to comparisons or associations; just as the multiplication table is learned, if it is ever learned at all. This can be done at an age when a child's reasoning powers ought not to be heavily taxed; and, under the direction of a judicious instructor, need not be a tedious or an irksome process.

It also assumes that a boy can parse simple English sentences. This he may be taught to do concurrently with the repetition of the Latin Accidence.

It does not profess to be a Manual of Latin Composition. When a boy has mastered the Lessons he cannot do better than begin the first part of Arnold. Meanwhile, a practical teacher will find, in the Examples, materials for retranslation, which he will abbreviate, expand, and vary at discretion, and will thus escape the annoyance arising from the dishonest use of a " Key." He will also, as his pupils proceed, explain more fully the use of the Subjunctive, the " sequence of tenses," the " *Oratio obliqua*," and other matters which are either wholly omitted or only partially explained in the following pages. I do not profess to have produced a book which supersedes the necessity for oral instruction.

The rules of Syntax are for the most part adopted from Zumpt ; the Examples, after the first five lessons, are, with few exceptions, extracted from classical authors ; and the " Invasions of Britain " are given in Cæsar's own words, with the omission of some few passages, possibly corrupt, certainly obscure, and of others which do not appear necessary to the narrative.

E. A.

August 25th, 1858.

ERRATA.

Page 4, line 3 from bottom, *for* sui, *read* tui.
„ 7, § 21, line 2, *for* and the, *read* and = the.
„ 9, § 29, „ 3, *for* Terribĭle, *read* Terribīle.
„ 9, § 31, „ 2, *dele* and = as in English.
„ 11, line 7, from bottom, *for* conspexerant, *read* conspexerat.
„ 15, „ 3, *for* ant, *read* aut.
„ 17, § 60, line 3, *for* miserescor, *read* miseresco.
„ 27, line 4, *for* endentity, *read* identity.

A

SECOND LATIN BOOK.

ACCENTUATION.

§ 1. Every syllable in Latin is either *long*, marked (¯),
or *short*, marked (˘).

A vowel before *two* consonants is generally *long*.

A diphthong is *long*.

A vowel before a vowel is generally *short*.

No rule can be given for the quantity (*i e.*, the length)
of a vowel before *one* consonant ; this must be learned by
practice.

§ 2. In dissyllables the accent is always on the *first*
syllable ; érat.

In words of more than two syllables, the accent is on
the *last but one* (the *penultimate*) when that is *long;* but,
when it is short, the accent falls on the *last but two* (the
antepenultimate).

In words of more than two syllables occurring in the
following lessons the quantity of the doubtful penultimate
is marked, except when it ought to be known from the
accidence.

LESSON I.

NOMINATIVE—ACCUSATIVE.

§ 3. In Latin, as in English, the NOMINATIVE case is
the subject of the sentence, and the verb agrees with it in
number and person.

§ 4. The nominative of pronouns is seldom expressed, as the termination of the verb shows what nominative must be supplied in English ; thus, "aud*it* =* *he, she,* or *it* hears." We say that this nominative is *understood.*

§ 5. The Latin ACCUSATIVE is the *immediate* object of a transitive verb, and is said to be *governed* by the verb.

§ 6. The arrangement of words in Latin differs essentially from their order in English ; and every attempt to translate the words in their Latin order, will be lost labour, producing, at best, nothing but bad English. To translate a Latin sentence, look first for the verb, and the verb will enable you to find the nominative. Then translate, 1. The nominative, 2. Words agreeing with the nominative or depending on it, 3. The verb with its adverbs, 4. The accusative, and the words agreeing with or depending upon it.

Claudo, 3 si, sum, *shut.*	*Timeo,* 2 *fear.*
Vinco, 3 ici, ictum, *conquer.*	*Capio,* 3 ēpi, aptum, *take.*
Diligo, 3 lexi, lectum, *love.*	*Accipio,* 3 cēpi, ceptum, *receive.*
Vendo, 3 dĭdi, dĭtum, *sell.*	*Suscipio,* „ *undertake.*
Monstro, 1¹† *show.*	*Scribo,* 3 *psi, ptum, write.*
Relinquo, 3 līqui, lictum, *leave behind.*	*Mitto,* 3 īsi, issum, *send.*
	Amitto, „ *lose.*

Servus, i, *slave.*	Miles, ĭtis, *soldier.*	Pater, ris, *father.*
Hostis, is, *enemy.*	Soror, ōris, *sister.*	Bellum, i, *war.*
Frater, ris, *brother.*	Amĭcus, i, *friend.*	Via, æ, *way.*
Agricŏla, æ, *husband-*	Libĕri, orum, *children.*	Arma, orum, *arms.*
Porta, æ, *gate.* [*man.*	Liber, ri, *book.*	Semper, *always.*
Mater, ris, *mother.*	Verbum, i, *word.*	Nunquam, *never.*
Epistŏla, æ, *letter.*	Tempŭs, ŏris, n., *time.*	Cur, *why.*

1. Servus portam claudit. 2. Miles hostes vicit. 3. Frater sorōrem reliquerat. 4. Semper te dilexi. 5. Amīcus libros vendet. 6. Monstra viam. 7. Servi claudent portam. 8. Arma capient milĭtes. 9. Cur me non monuisti ? 10. Nos misit. 11. Mater reliquerat liberos. 12. Hostes me timent. 13. Verba audite. 14. Agricŏla nunquam tempus amittit. 15. Epistŏlam acceperam. 16. Arma capiebant. 17. Sorōres epistŏlas scribebant. 18. Amicum amittent. 19. Nos bellum suscepimus. 20. Hostes miles vicerat.

---

* This sign (=) means "*is* or *are translated by.*"

† A small figure refers to Appendix I., which follows the Lessons.

LESSON II.

ADJECTIVES—PARTICIPLES.

§ 7. An ADJECTIVE is of the same gender, number, and case, as the noun or personal pronoun which it qualifies; and is said to *agree* with that noun or pronoun. POSSESSIVE pronouns follow the same rule. So also do PARTICIPLES, which are verbal adjectives. With participles a personal pronoun is very frequently *understood*.

§ 8. A Latin adjective is often used alone where we require a noun with it. It is then said to be used *absolutely*, and is to be parsed as a noun. When in the masculine, we must, in translating, supply the noun *man;* when in the neuter, *thing.* Thus, " *malus* "=" a bad man ;" " *turpe* " =" a *disgraceful* thing." Very often however a neuter adjective is best translated by an English noun of the same meaning ; thus, " *malum* "=" an *evil, a misfortune.*"

§ 9. A Demonstrative adjective used *absolutely* (*i.e.,* without a noun) becomes a personal pronoun ; thus, " hic," " ille," " is,"=" *he ;*" " hujus," " illius," " ejus," =" *his,*" &c.

Meus, *my.*	Omnis, *all.*	Crudēlis, *cruel.*
Noster, *our.*	Fidēlis, *faithful.*	Hic, *this.*
Tuus, *your.*	Carus, *dear.*	Inutīlis, *useless.*
Vester, *your,* pl.	Fortis, *brave.*	Parcus, *thrifty.*
Suus,[4] *his, her, their.*	Brevis, *short.*	Invītus, *unwilling.*
Multus, *much,* pl. *many*	Ignāvus, *lazy.*	

1. Servus fidēlis portam clausit tuam. 2. Fortis miles crudēlem hostem vincet. 3. Agricŏlæ nostri non timebunt hostes. 4. Bonus viam monstrabit. 5. Pater tuus epistŏlas accipit multas. 6. Omnia mea amisi. 7. Carus amicus fidelissĭmum servum miserat. 8. Soror ejus brevem scripsit epistŏlam. 9. Servos monebo. 10. Cur hæc reliquisti? 11. Hunc timebat soror mea. 12. Omne tempus ignāvi amiserunt servi. 13. [2]Nostri arma capiunt. 14. Non sumus crudēles. 15. Patres vestri bella crudēlia suscipiebant. 16. Libros inutīles parcus agricŏla vendidit. 17. Epistŏla tua brevis est. 18. Carissĭmum fratrem suum mater mea amiserat. 19. Verba mea tu nunquam audies. 20.[3]Invītus omnes relīquit libros.

LESSON III.

GENITIVE.

§ 10. The primary meaning of the GENITIVE Case is possession; and it then = the English *possessive* or the preposition *of*; thus, "fratr*is* mei epistola"="*my brother's* letter;" "Milit*um* arma"="the arms *of* the soldiers."

§ 11. But the genitive also expresses other relations between nouns; and frequently = other prepositions, such as, *from, for*, &c.; thus, "Requies labor*um*"="rest *from* labours;" "Benefic*ii* gratia"="gratitude *for* a favour." The noun in the genitive is said to be *governed* by the other noun.

§ 12. The genitive is used to express the *whole* of which anything is a *part;* and is, in this way, governed by *pars*, or a word of like meaning; by comparatives, superlatives, and interrogatives; or by words denoting number. These governing words are called *Partitives;* and the genitive usually = *of*.

§ 13. The genitive is also governed by a neuter adjective signifying *quantity*, and = the case of that adjective; thus, "*Multum* tempŏr*is* amisit"="He has lost *much time*."

§ 14. Again, the genitive is governed by some adjectives which require the addition of a noun or pronoun to complete the sense. Such adjectives are those which express *partaking, desiring, experiencing, knowing, remembering, being full*, and their *contraries*. This genitive *usually* = *of;* thus, "cupidus gloriæ"="desirous *of* glory;" "ignārus viæ"="ignorant *of* the way."

Urbs, is, *city*.	Cupĭdus, *desirous*.	Quantus, *how great, how much.*
Labor, ōris, *labour*.	Ignārus, *ignorant*.	
Pecunia, æ, *money*.	Jucundus, *pleasant*.	Tantus, *so great, so much.*
Dives, ĭtis, *rich*.		

1. Servi fidēles claudebant urbis portas.   2. Cæsăris milĭtes arma capient.   3. Divĭtis agricŏlæ frater multum pecuniæ amisit.   4. Sorōris tuæ servus viam monstravit.   5. Non omnes sumus cupĭdi gloriæ.   6. Te semper amavit fratris sui amīcus.   7. Quantum tempŏris omnes amittent!   8. Cur non vendidisti parci agricŏlæ inutĭles libros?   9. Bellum suscipiant hostes armorum ignāri.   10. Ignāvi

servi frater non misit epistŏlam. 11. Audi patris mei verba. 12. Semper cupĭdi gloriæ fuistis. 13. Hostes invīti arma ceperunt. 14. Jucundissĭma est requies labōrum. 15. Omnia vincit labor. 16. Parcōrum agricolārum labor non inutĭlis est. 17. Cæsăris milĭtes arma sua nunquam vendent. 18. Agricŏlæ soror epistŏlam scripsit brevissĭmam. 19. Fortissimi milites Cæsăris ceperant hostium urbem. 20. Tantum labŏris non invitus suscepi.

LESSON IV.

DATIVE.

§ 15. The DATIVE Case is—
1. The *remote* object of the action expressed by a transitive verb ; thus, " Dăre qd. *cui.*"=" to give *aby.* athg., or to give athg. *to aby.;*" " imponĕre qd. *cui.*"= " to place athg. *on aby.;*" " suadēre qd. *cui.*"=" to persuade *aby. of* a thing."

⁎ *The following abbreviations will hereafter be employed,* qm. *for* aliquem, qd. *for* aliquid, cui. *for* alicui, quo. *for* aliquo ; aby. *for* anybody, athg. *for* anything.

2. The *immediate* object of almost all intransitive verbs, especially of those compounded with prepositions, many of which = *English* transitive verbs ; thus, " parcĕre *cui.*" =" to spare *aby.;*" " nocēre *cui.*"=" to injure *aby.;*" " prodesse *cui.*"=" to do good *to aby.;*" " subvenīre *cui.*"=" to assist *aby.*"

3. It is governed by adjectives expressing the idea of *advantage, likeness, equality, pleasantness, suitableness,* or *ease,* and their *opposites ;* thus, " similis *cui.*"=" like *aby.* or *athg.;*" aptum *cui.*"=" fit *for aby.* or *athg.;*" " utile *cui.*"=" useful to *aby.* or *athg.*"

§ 16. From the foregoing examples it will be seen, that the dative generally = *to* or *for ;* but often = some other preposition, and not unfrequently = the English accusative.

Do, 1 dĕdi, dătum, *give.*	Prosum, fui, futūrus, *do good.*
Vĕnio, 4 vēni, ventum, *come.*	Desum, „ *am wanting.*
Subvenio, 4 „ *assist.*	Adfĕro, tŭli, lātum, *bring.*
Noceo, 2 *injure.*	Suadeo, 2 si, sum, *persuade.*

1. Mihi viam monstrate. 2. Libros filio meo dedisti
multos. 3. Servus fidēlis domĭno subveniet. 4. Bonus
omnibus prodest. 5. Venies amīcis carus. 6. Hoc bellum
multis nocebit. 7. Labor tuus inutĭlis mihi adtŭlit nihil
boni. 8. Libĕri non sunt patri simĭles. 9. Cæsar militibus suis multum dedit pecuniæ. 10. Libros mihi inutĭles tibi non vendam. 11. Sorōris tuæ epistŏla nobis
fuit jucundissima. 12. Divĭtis agricŏlæ fratri hoc sua-
debo. 13. Dent mihi pecuniam. 14. Libri illi non sunt
temporibus apti. 15. Urbem hostibus crudēles vendide-
rant milĭtes. 16. Verba mihi desunt. 17. Hæc jucunda
sunt divitibus, nobis inutilia. 18. Cur non profuit amīcis? 19. Quantum mihi attulisti pecuniæ. 20. Non
mihi, non fratri hoc suadebis. 21. Tempus deest mihi.

LESSON V.

ABLATIVE.

§ 17. The primary use of the ABLATIVE case is to
express the *cause*, *manner*, or *instrument*, of an action, and
it then = one of the prepositions *by*, *with*, *from*, *in*, &c.

§ 18. A noun *and* adjective in the ablative are used to
qualify another noun, either with or without the verb *sum*.
This ablative = the preposition *of*, thus, " vir *summa
integritate*"="a man *of* the highest integrity." The
genitive is used in the same way; and such a phrase is
called the ablative (or genitive) of *quality*.

§ 19. The ablative is governed by the adjectives *dignus,
indignus, præditus, contentus, extorris, fretus*, and *liber ;* and
also by *natus* and other words signifying *born* or *sprung
from ;* thus, " *vita* indignus "="unworthy *of* life ;"
" natus *Dea* "="born *of* a goddess."

§ 20. The ablative *or* genitive is governed by adjectives
expressing the idea of *abundance* or *want ;* thus, " plenus
vino or *vini* "="full *of* wine."

Virtūs, ūtis, f., *virtue.*	Benevolentia, *good will*	Infimus, *lowest.*
Restis, is, f., *rope.*	Culpa, *fault.*	Summus, *highest.*
Manus, us, f., *hand*	Dolus, i, *fraud.*	Fretus, *relying.*
Classis, is, f., *fleet.*	Nemo, ĭnis, *nobody.*	Contentus, *content.*
Res, rēi, f., *thing, fact.*	Ingenium, *capacity.*	Natus, *born.*
Nomen, ĭnis, n., *name.*	Plenus, *full.*	Prædĭtus, *endowed.*

1. Patres nostri virtūte non dolis hostes vincebant. 2.

Agricŏlæ servus clausit portam reste. 3. Carissima soror manu sua scripserat epistŏlam. 4. Milites classe venient. 5. Re, non nomĭne, amĭcus est pater. 6. Brutus, vir summo ingenio, urbem relīquit. 7. Cur facis rem parvam magnam verbis tuis. 8. Verba patris tui plena sunt benevolentiæ. 9. Agricŏla iste, homo infima turpitudĭne, servos hostibus vendidit. 10. Fratris mei amĭcus hunc librum scripsit manu sua. 11. Urbs fuit hostibus plena. 12. Pater tuus, vir summa virtūte, illum suscipiet labōrem. 13. Quod verbum non fuit benevolentia plenum? 14. Omnes amīces culpa tua amittes. 15. Armis et virtūte vincent nostri omnia. 16. Fretus virtūte milĭtum Cæsar non timebit dolos hostium. 17. Nemĭni profuisti; vita es indignus. 18. Parvo contentus nunquam fui pecuniæ cupĭdus. 19. Natus bono patre, fuit ipse infima turpitudine. 20. Prœdĭtus fuit Cæsar summo ingenio.

₊ *Henceforward the English of words not in the foregoing lists must be looked for in the vocabulary.*

LESSON VI.

PASSIVE VOICE—PREPOSITIONS.

§ 21. In a sentence constructed with a verb in the PASSIVE voice, the *agent* (*i.e.*, the *person* who does) is regularly in the ablative governed by the preposition *a*; but with tenses compounded of the *past* participle the dative *may* be used, and with the *future* participle the dative *must* be used; thus, "inventum est a *quo*., or (sometimes) inventum est *cui*."="it has been found out *by aby*." "inveniendum est *cui*."="it is to be found out *by aby*."

§ 21. The remote object of the verb in the active voice remains in the same case with the passive voice and the same preposition; thus, "qd. datur *cui*."="athg. is given *to aby*." "qd. eripitur *cui*."=athg. is taken *from aby*."

§ 22. No verb which does not in the active voice govern the accusative of the *person*, can be used in the first or second persons of the passive; thus, we cannot say, respondeor, *I am answered*.

§ 23. Such verbs are however used *impersonally* in the

passive, with the person in the case of the remote object, and = the English passive of the personal verb; thus, *"mihi* respondetur*"="I am* answered," *"vobis* respondetur*"="ye are* answered."

§ 24. An impersonal verb in the passive followed by no case = the indefinite English *it* with the *passive,* or = the indefinite *we, they, people,* with the *active;* thus, "pugnatum est*"="it was fought,"* or, "*we, they,* &c. fought."

§ 25. A PREPOSITION stands regularly, either, 1. Before the noun it governs, 2. Before the adjective agreeing with that noun, or 3. Before the genitive governed by that noun.

§ 26. For the meanings and government of prepositions see the Accidence.⁵

1. Utilĭs hic liber ab amīco est mihi datus. 2. Urbis porta fidelibus a servis claudebitur. 3. Ripa erat acūtis sudibus ab hostibus munita. 4. Hostibus a nostris nocebatur. 5. Pugnatum est ab utrisque⁶ acrĭter. 6. Accessum est ad Britanniam. 7. Hoc Cæsari nuntiatur ab exploratoribus. 8. Omnes naves cum castris una munitiōne conjunctæ sunt. 9. Arboribus introĭtus erant præclusi. 10. Munitiōni castrorum tempus relictum est. 11. Multitudĭne navium perterrĭti sunt hostes. 12. Hæc a compluribus ad Cæsărem deferebantur. 13. Complūres minōres insŭlæ objectæ⁷ existimantur. 14. Sub ocŭlis omnium ac pro castris dimicatur. 15. Flumen pedibus transiri potest. 16. Itum est in viscĕra terræ. 17. Densi funduntur ab æthĕre nimbi. 18. Jacĕre lapides post terga jubemur. 19. Me misit in arva suo quondam regnäta parenti. 20. Illa vetus casa vertitur in templum.

LESSON VII.

GERUNDS, SUPINES, PARTICIPLES, ABLATIVE ABSOLUTE.

§ 27. The GERUNDS with the infinitive make up the verbal noun, which is thus declined. N. *Amare;* G. *Amandi;* D. and Abl. *Amando;* Acc. *Amare* and (after prepositions) *Amandum.*

§ 28. But instead of the gerund of a *transitive* verb the future participle passive is very frequently used, in agreement with the noun or pronoun which would be governed by the gerund. In this construction, we must translate as though the gerund were used; thus, "cupĭdo urb*is* condend*æ*," *or* "cupĭdo urb*em* condend*i*"="a desire *of building* a city."

§ 29. The SUPINE in *um* is a verbal noun used only after verbs of motion; that in *u* after adjectives; thus, "Eo lus*um*"="I am going to play;" "Terribĭle vis*u*"="*Athg.* terrible to see."

§ 30. There is no PAST *participle* of the active voice in Latin. Hence if we would say, "Cæsar, *having conquered his enemies*, returned to Italy," we must use the "CASE ABSOLUTE," and say, "Cæsar, his *enemies having been conquered*, returned to Italy." Now, in Latin, the *Ablative* is employed for the Case Absolute, and the sentence is, "Cæsar *victis hostibus*, in Italiam rediit."

§ 31. The past participle of a deponent verb *has* an active signification, and = as in English; thus, "Cæsar hæc *locutus* rediit "="Cæsar, *having spoken* these (words) returned." This participle very often = the English present.

§ 32. The *future participle passive* (apart from its use above mentioned) signifies *necessity* or *duty;* and the verb sum is almost always to be understood in connection with it, if not expressed. The agent, if expressed, is, unless the verb govern a dative, always in the dative, which = the preposition *by;* "Domus ædificanda est *mihi*"="A house is to be built *by* me."

§ 33. But a sentence of this kind is better translated by turning the verb into the active voice; and when the participle is used impersonally in the neuter it *must* be so translated. To do this, the *dative* of the agent = the English *nominative*, the Latin *nominative* = the English *accusative*, and the *participle* with *est, sunt,* &c. = *must, have to,* &c. with the *infinitive active*, thus :—

Domus ædificanda est mihi = I *must, have to*, build a house.
Scribendum est tibi = You *must, have to*, write.
Scribenda est tibi epistola = You *must, have to*, write a letter.
Parcendum est victis = *We, you, aby.*, must spare the conquered.

§ 34. In compound tenses the auxiliary *sum* is very frequently omitted, so that it requires a little attention to determine whether a participle is used as an adjective or is part of a tense. To ascertain this, observe whether or not the following verb is preceded by a conjunction; if it is, the participle requires for its complement the proper tense of *sum;* if it is not, the participle is an adjective agreeing with a noun or pronoun; thus, "Hostes *fusi fugatique* sunt"="The enemies *were routed and* put to flight." " Hostes *fusi* effugerunt "=" The *routed* enemies fled."

§ 35. A past participle passive agreeing with the *accusative*, frequently = either, 1. The same participle *active* agreeing with the *nominative*, or, 2. A separate *verb* and *conjunction;* thus, "Oppidum *captum* incendit "= "*Having taken* the town he set it on fire," or, " *He took* the town *and* set it on fire."

1. Propter anni tempus belli gerendi facultātem non habuit. 2. Nostris omnibus occupatis, hostes discesserunt. 3. Magna militum multitudine coacta, ad castra venerunt. 4. Omni ex relĭquis partibus demesso frumento, pars una erat relĭqua. 5. Prædæ faciendæ facultas dabatur. 6. Commisso prælio, hostes terga verterunt. 7. Militibus de navibus desiliendum et cum hostibus erat pugnandum. 8. Qua re nunciata, Cæsar omnem ex castris equitātum misit. 9. Moriendum est omnibus. 10. Cuncta prius tentanda ; sed immedicabile vulnus ense recīdendum est. 11. Hostium ducem cecīdit, cæssumque spoliavit. 12. In comparandis amīcis magna est adhibenda diligentia. 13. Magnus ibi numĕrus pecŏris repertus, multique mortales in fuga sunt interfecti. 14. In agris vastandis incendiisque faciendis hostibus nocebatur.

LESSON VIII.

RELATIVE.

§ 36. The Latin RELATIVE agrees with its antecedent in gender, number, and person. When the relative has more than one antecedent of different genders it is in the plural, and of the masculine gender rather than the feminine ; but when it refers to things without life it is usually neuter. When a whole sentence is the antecedent the relative is neuter ; and *id quod = a circumstance which* is frequently used for *quod*. The antecedents *is, ea, id,* &c. are *very often* omitted. *Quod* and *quæ* (neut. pl.) then = *what.*

§ 37. The *case* of the relative is ascertained as in English.

The antecedent is sometimes *repeated* in the relative clause, and is then not to be translated; thus, "Erant omnino itinera duo, quibus *itineribus,*" &c.="There were in all two roads by *which,*" &c.

§ 38. The relative clause, with or without the antecedent in it, sometimes stands first, and then, in the principal clause, the antecedent is usually represented by a demonstrative. In translating such a sentence, *begin* with the clause containing the demonstrative and supply the antecedent.

"Quas ad me dedisti *(eas)* accepi literas "="I have received the letter which you sent me." "*Quæ* gravissime afflictæ erant *naves, earum* materia," &c.="The timber of *those ships which* had been most seriously damaged."

Antecedent.	Relative.		
Tantus	.. Quantus	=	*as great as.*
Talis	.. Qualis	=	*such as.*
Idem	.. Qui	=	*the same as.*
Tot	.. Quot	=	*as many as.*
Toties	.. Quoties	=	*as many times as.*

1. In medio est insŭla, quæ appellatur Mona. 2. Insŭla natūra triquetra; cujus unum latus est contra Galliam. 3. Easdem copias, quas ante, relīquit. 4. Nacti sunt locum, quem jam ante præparaverant. 5. In castris hostium tabŭlæ repertæ sunt, litĕris Græcis confectæ, quibus in tabūlis ratio confecta erat. 6. Ex his longe sunt humanissimi qui Cantium incŏlunt. 7. Qui erant in statiōne pro castris acrĭter pugnaverunt. 8. Cæsar ad flumen Tamĕsin exercĭtum duxit, quod flumen uno omnīno loco pedibus transiri potest. 9. Tanti fuerunt fluctus, quantos nunquam antea videram. 10. Quos laborantes conspexerant, iis subsidia submittebat. 11. Quod dixisti verum est. 12. Coram, quem quæritis, adsum. 13. Quibus rebus cognĭtis, principes Britanniæ inter se sunt collocūti. 14. Qui decĭmæ legiōnis aquĭlam ferebat, "Desilite" inquit "commilitōnes." 15. Quas dedimus, certe terras habitare sinemus.[9]

LESSON IX.

ACCUSATIVE AND INFINITIVE.

§ 39. The INFINITIVE MOOD preceded by an ACCUSA-
TIVE is the *object* after verbs of *seeing, hearing, knowing,
thinking, feeling,* &c. ; but the *subject* to *est, &c.* with an
adjective, to impersonal verbs as *constat,* and to a passive
verb used impersonally, as *intelligitur.*[10] The accusative
and infinitive = the nominative and indicative preceded
by the conjunction *that.*[11]

§ 40.

$$\text{Dicit } se \left\{ \begin{array}{l} \textit{esse} \\ \textit{fuisse} \\ \textit{fore} \end{array} \right\} \text{beatum} = \text{He says } \textit{that he} \left\{ \begin{array}{l} \textit{is} \\ \textit{was} \\ \textit{will be} \end{array} \right\} \text{happy.}$$

$$\text{Dixit } se \left\{ \begin{array}{l} \textit{esse} \\ \textit{fuisse} \\ \textit{fore} \end{array} \right\} \text{beatum} = \text{He said } \textit{that he} \left\{ \begin{array}{l} \textit{was} \\ \textit{had been} \\ \textit{would be} \end{array} \right\} \text{happy.}$$

" Ad salutem civium *inventas esse leges* constat " =
" It is evident *that laws were invented* for the welfare of
the citizens."

§ 41. After verbs of *hoping, promising,* and *undertaking,*
the *future* infinitive is generally used, and *may* = the
English infinitive *present.*

" Speravit *se victurum* " = " He hoped *to live; or that
he would live.*"

1. Dicis te libros legere.   2. Dicis te libros legisse.
3. Dicis te libros lecturum esse.   4. Dixisti te libros legere.
5. Dixisti te libros legisse.   6. Dixisti te libros lecturum
(esse).   7. Dicis hostes a te vinci.   8. Dicis hostes a te
victos (esse).   9. Dixisti hostes a te vinci.   10. Dixisti
hostes a te victos.   11. Promīsit puella se ventūram.   12.
Ad committendum prælium aliēnum esse tempus arbitratus
est.   13. Cæsar legiōnes equitatumque revocari jubet.   14.
Intellectum est equĭtes magno cum perícŭlo dimicare.
15. Animadvertit ad altĕram flumĭnis ripam magnas esse
copias hostium instructas.   16. Pollicentur sese ei dedituros   atque   imperata   facturos.   17. Commius   venit,
quem[12] supra demonstraveram a Cæsare in Britanniam
præmissum.   18. Has occupatiōnes sibi Britanniæ ante-
ponendas (esse) non judicabat.   19. Hostibus nostris inde
subministrata auxilia intelligebat.   20. Satis   se   et   ad

laudem et[13] ad utilītātem profectum arbitrātur. 21.
Breviores esse, quam in continente, noctes videbamus.

LESSON X.

SUBJUNCTIVE MOOD.

§ 42. The SUBJUNCTIVE connected with a preceding
verb[14] by *" ut,"*[15] meaning *in order that,* (or by its ne-
gative *" ne," in order that not,*)= *may, might, &c.* or *the
infinitive.*[16]

" Edimus *ut vivamus,"*=" we eat *to live,"* or *" that we
may live."* " Cura *ne* id *facias "*=" take care *not to do*
that."

§ 43. After a verb of *fearing,* the subjunctive preceded
by *" ut "* or *" ne "*= the *future* indicative. " Vereor *ne "*
=" I fear *aby. will ;"* " Vereor *ut "*=" I fear *aby. will
not."*

§ 44. The subjunctive with " *qui* " before it often = the
infinitive. This·*qui* stands for *ut ille,* or *ut illi,* meaning
in order that he, &c.

" Miserunt legātos qui pacem *peterent "*=" they sent
ambassadors *to sue* for peace ;" which they may or may
not have sued for : " qui *petierunt "* would mean that they
actually did so.

§ 45. The subjunctive with *quin* = *but that, that,* and
the *indicative,* or, after verbs of *hindering,*= *from* with the
English *verbal noun.* So also with *quominus,* and sometimes *ne.*

" Vix inhiberi potuit *quin* saxa *jaceret "*=" he could
scarcely be restrained *from throwing* stones."

§ 46. In *hypothetical propositions*[17] the subjunctive of
the past tenses = *would,* &c.

§ 47. In most other cases the subjunctive = the indicative.

1. Ad eum legāti venerunt qui se excusarent. 2. Hoc
quum magna voce dixisset, ex navi se projēcit. 3. Quæ
imperavisset sese facturos pollicĭti sunt. 4. Tanta tempestas coorta est ut nulla navium cursum tenere posset.
5. Demonstraverunt quanta prædæ faciendæ facultas da-

retur, si Romānos castris expulissent. 6. Labieno scribit ut, quam plurĭmas[18] posset naves, instituat. 7. Ea celeritāte milĭtes ierunt, ut hostes impĕtum sustinere non possent. 8. Cassivellaunus, ut supra demonstravimus copias dimīsit. 9. Petunt ut in civitātem mittat qui imperium obtineat. 10. His impĕrat ut de improvīso castra adoriantur. 11. Huic mandat, uti, exploratis omnibus rebus, ad se quam primum revertatur. 12. Quanta esset insŭlæ magnitūdo reperire non poterat. 13. Nondum, ut peregrīnum viseret orbem, in liquĭdas pinus descenderat undas. 14. Dixit non esse dubium quin totīus Galliæ plurĭmum possent.[19] 15. Hi seditiōsa oratiōne multitudĭnem deterrent ne frumentum confĕrant. 16. Ne fratris supplicio amīci sui anĭmum offenderet, verebatur. 17. Cæsar ejus dextram prendit; rogat (ut) finem orandi faciat. 18. Postulavit ne quam[20] multitudĭnem homĭnum trans Rhenum transduceret. 19. Nonnulli, ut timōris suspiciōnem vitarent, remanebant. 20. Cæsar suis imperavit ne quod omnīno telum in hostes rejicerent. 21. Non abest suspicio, ut Helvetii arbitrantur, quin ipse sibi mortem consciverit.

LESSON XI.

TIME, PLACE, &c.

§ 48. The Ablative expresses the time *when*, or *within what time;* the Accusative, the time *how long.* "*In*" with the acc. of time ="*for;*" "*abhinc*" with acc. or abl.="*ago.*"

§ 49. The name of a town *at which* an event happens is in the *genitive,* if of the *first* or *second* declension and of the *singular* number; *otherwise* in the *ablative.*

§ 50. The name of the town *to which* is in the *accusative;* of that *from which* in the *ablative.*

§ 51. *Domus* and *rus* follow the rules for the names of towns.

§ 52. "Ruri"="*in the* country;" "humi"="*on the* ground;" "belli"="*at* war;" "militiæ"="*in the* field;" "mille passus"="*a mile;*" "quinque millia passuum"="*five miles.*"

1. In fines Helvetiorum die septĭmo pervĕnit. 2. Quorum virtus fuerat domi militiæque cognĭta. 3. Non
fuerat mihi dubium quin te visurus essem Tarenti ant
Brundusii. 4. Forte evēnit ut essemus ruri. 5. Fuit eo
tempŏre omni Neapŏli.²¹ 6. Abiit Roma; profectus est in
Siciliam; tres annos Syracūsis habitavit. 7. Veni Athēnas,
neque²² quisquam ibi me agnōvit. 8. Damnatus cessit
Athēnis et Rhodum se contŭlit. 9. Me mea domo ex-
pulisti. 10. Ab his cognoscit, non longe ex eo loco oppĭdum Cassivellauni abesse. 11. Circiter millia passuum
sex ab eo loco progressus, aperto ac plano litŏre naves
eonstituit. 12. Orta luce, sub sinistra Britanniam relictam
conspexit. 13. Postridie ejus diēi mane milĭtes equitesque
in expeditiōnem misit, ut eos, qui fugerant, persequerentur. 14. Hibernia dimidio minor est, ut æstimatur,
quam Britannia; sed pari spatio transmissus atque²³ ex
Gallia in Britanniam. 15. De quibus insŭlis nonnulli
scripserunt dies continuos triginta sub bruma esse noctem.
16. Eo die hostes sequitur, et millia passuum tria ab
eorum castris castra ponit.

LESSON XII.

APPOSITION—INTERROGATIONS.

§ 53. Nouns signifying the same person or thing are in
the same case; as are also the words that ask and answer
a question.

§ 54. "Urbs Roma"="the city of Rome;" "Insula
Britannia"="the island of Britain."

§ 55. Substantive verbs of *becoming, being, seeming*, and
Passive verbs of *naming, making, calling, deeming*, take
the same case after them as before them.²⁴

§ 56. "Ne"²⁶ appended to a word denotes a question.
"Num" expects the answer "no;" but after a verb of
asking = "whether."

"Utrum"—"num," or the appended "ne," followed by
"an"="whether,"—"or;" but the former word is frequently omitted when the double question follows a verb.

1. Consŭlem misimus, virum fortissimum cum exercĭtu.

2. Virtūtis magistri philosŏphi inventi sunt, qui summum malum dolōrem dicerent. 3. Prætor postea factus est et consul. 4. Bellum ita suscipiatur ut nihil aliud nisi pax videatur quæsīta.[7] 5. Quis ergo adfuit? Frater, inquit, uxōris meæ. 6. Malum mihi videtur mors. Iisne, qui mortui sunt vel quibus moriendum est? Utrisque. 7. Quæro num quis[20] ante te tam fuerit nefarius, qui id fecerit?[25] ut sciamus, utrum vetĕrum facinŏrum sis imitator, an inventor novorum. 8. Satisne igĭtur videor vim verborum tenere? 9. Dubĭto, æquum sit an inīquum. 10. Proxĭma nocte castra movit, ut quam primum intelligere posset, utrum apud eos officium an timor plus valeret. 11. Mortemne mihi minitaris[27] an exilium? 12. Publium Rufum, Legātum, cum eo præsidio quod satis esse arbitrabatur, portum tenere jussit. 13. Consul, hoc feci. 14. Quis est qui hoc fecerit? 15. Unde venis? 16. Quo abis? 17. Quo te agis?[28] 18. Quid agis? 19. Quid tibi vis? 20. Cur huc venisti? 21. Defendi rempublicam adolescens, non desĕram senex.

LESSON XIII.

OTHER USES OF THE GENITIVE.

§ 57. The genitive is governed by *Sum* or *Fio* in the sense of *belonging to*, being the *business*, *duty*, or *mark* of; thus, " *Regis est* "=" it is *the duty of* a king;" " *Boni pastoris est* "=" it is *the mark of* a good shepherd;". " *Esse sui juris* "=" to be *one's own master*." But instead of the genitive of personal pronouns, *meum*, *tuum*, &c. are used; " *Tuum est* "=" it is your business."

§ 58. The genitive is the remote object after verbs of *accusing*, *condemning*, *acquitting*, *and admonishing*, and denotes the charge, *offence*, or *punishment*; thus, " Accusare *qm. cujus* "=" to accuse *aby. of athg.*;" " Damnāre *qm. capitis* "=" to condemn *aby. to death*."

§ 59. This genitive appears to be governed by *crimine*, *nomine*, or *judicio* understood, and these words are frequently inserted. The *ablative* with *de* is also used for the genitive. Verbs of admonishing take the *accusative* of neuter demonstratives.

§ 60. The genitive (and sometimes the accusative) is the *immediate* object of *memini, reminiscor, recordor,* and *ob-liviscor,* and also of *misereor* and *miserescor.*

§ 61. The impersonals *pudet, piget, pœnitet, tædet,* and *miseret,* govern the *accusative* of the *person* and the *genitive* of the *thing;* thus, " Pudet *qm. cujus* "=" *aby.* is ashamed of *athg.*"

§ 62. *Interest* governs the genitive of the person, but *mea, tua,* &c. in the ablative instead of *mei, tui,* &c. *Refert* takes the pronouns in the ablative, but very rarely. governs the genitive. " Interest *Cæsaris* "=" it concerns *Cæsar.*" " *Tua* interest *or* refert "=" it is *your* business."

§ 63. *Potior* governs the *genitive* or *ablative.*

§ 64. The genitive is governed by adverbs of *place, time,* and *quantity.* (See § 13.)

§ 65. The genitive, generally of an adjective, as *tanti, quanti,* &c. denotes the *indefinite* value or cost.

1. Est boni consŭlis, non solum[29] videre quid agatur, verum etiam providere quid futurum sit. 2. Nunquam tam amens fuisset, ut, si se ambĭtu commaculavisset, ambĭtus alterum accusaret. 3. Suis eum certis propriis-que criminibus accusabo. 4. Fratris me hic annŭlus commonuit. 5. Oro te, eam moneas de testamento. 6. Reminiscatur et vetĕris incommŏdi Popŭli Romāni et pristĭnæ virtūtis Helvetiorum. 7. Si vetĕris contumeliæ oblivisci vellet, num etiam recentium injuriarum mem-oriam deponere posset? 8. Ipse certe agnoscet, et cum alĭquo dolōre flagitiorum suorum recordabitur. 9. Nemo jam, neque tui, neque tuorum liberorum, quos tu in eges-tāte atque in solitudĭne reliquisti, misereri potest. 10. Ea perturbatio est omnium rerum, ut suæ quemque[30] fortūnæ maxime pœniteat. 11. Tu mecum in gratiam redeas,[31] si scias quam me pudeat nequitiæ tuæ, cujus te ipsum non pudet. 12. Si talium civium vos, judĭces, tædet, ostendite. 13. Per tres potentissimos ac fir-missimos populos totīus Galliæ sese potiri posse sperant. 14. Sumus natūra studiosissimi honestātis : cujus si quasi lumen aliquod aspexerimus, nihil est quod, ut eo potiamur, non parati simus et ferre et perpĕti. 15. O Dii immortales ! ubinam gentium sumus? in qua urbe vivimus? quam rem-publicam habemus? 16. Postridie ejus diēi iter ab Helvetiis avertit ac Bibracte ire contendit. 17. Satis habeo

negotii in sanandis vulneribus, quæ sunt imposïta pro-
vinciæ. 18. Cupio excurrere in Græciam ; magni intĕrest
Ciceronis me intervenire discenti. 19. Permagni nostra
intĕrest te esse Romæ. 20. Nullo in loco frumentum
tanti fuit quanti iste[32] æstimavit. 21. Non quantum
quisque prosit sed quanti quisque sit, ponderandum est.
22. Eum semper equïdem, ut scis, dilexi, sed quotidie
pluris facio.

LESSON XIV.

OTHER USES OF THE DATIVE.

§ 66. The dative is sometimes used for the genitive when
the governing noun is a part of the body, as " *caput* "; or
anything so closely connected with the governing noun as
to form a necessary part of it, as " *nomen*," " *animus*," &c.

§ 67. A dative is used after the verbs " *sum*," " *do*,"
" *duco*," &c. where *we* use a noun in apposition, or one
connected by " *as*," &c. This dative expresses a *purpose,
cause, effect,* or *destination.*

§ 68. The dative with " *est*," " *sunt*," &c.=" *have*." In
this construction the dative = the English nominative ;
" *est*," " *sunt*," &c. = the corresponding tense of " *have* ";
and the Latin nominative = the English accusative ; thus,
" *qd. est cui.*"=" *aby. has athg.*" " *Suppetit*"=" *there is
enough,*" is construed in the same manner.

§ 69. The dative is the *immediate* object of the impersonals *libet, licet, liquet, convenit,* (it suits,) *expedit, con-
tingit, accidit,* and others of similar signification.

§ 70. "Pollicïtus est, caput *Italiæ omni* Capuam fore "
=" he promised that Capua should be the head *of* all
Italy." " Syracūsis est fons, *cui* nomen Arethūsa "=
" there is at Syracuse a fountain the name *of* which is
Arethusa." " Est mihi *voluptati*"=" it is a pleasure to
me." " Hoc erit mihi *curæ* "=" this will be *a care* to me,
or, I will take care of this." " Erit mihi *usui*"=" it will
be *of use* to me." " Illud mihi *dono* dedit"=" he gave
me that *as a gift.*" " *Dare cui. crimini*"=" to *impute to
aby. as a fault.*" " *Est mihi liber*"=" *I have a book ;*
" *Erant mihi libri* duo"=" *I had* two *books.* " *Suppetit
cibus* multo labōre querentibus"=" *they have food enough*

who seek it with great labour." "*Licet mihi ire*"="*it is permitted me to go,* or, *I may go.*" "*Licuit mihi ire*"= "*it was permitted,* &c. or, *I might have gone.*" "*Obvius* or *obviam ire cui.*"="*to go out to meet aby.*" Venire *auxilio cui.*"="*to come to the assistance of aby.*"

1. Funĕra sunt pro cultu[3][3] Gallorum magnifĭca et sumptuosa; omniaque, quæ vivis cordi fuisse arbitrantur, in ignem infĕrunt, etiam animalia. 2. Magno sibi usui fore arbitrabatur si modo insŭlam adisset, genus hominum perspexisset, loca, portus, adĭtus, cognovisset. 3. Legātos ad eum miserunt, qui dicerent, sibi esse in animo sine ullo maleficio iter per provinciam facere. 4. Dixit Ariovistus, amicitiam Populi Romani sibi ornamento et præsidio, non detrimento, esse oportere, idque se ea spe petiisse. 5. Hoc fecerunt ne qua legio alteri legiōni subsidio venire posset. 6. Mihi autem non minōri curæ est, qualis respublica post mortem meam futūra sit, quam qualis hodie sit. 7. Non is solum gratus debet esse, qui accēpit beneficium, verum etiam is cui potestas accipiendi fuit. 8. Tibi omnia suppĕtunt, quæ consĕqui ingenio aut usu homines, aut diligentia possunt. 9. Mihi erit maxime curæ, ne quid fiat secus quam volumus. 10. Rogant eum legāti, ut ejus voluntāte sibi iter per Provinciam facere liceat. 11. Licet nemĭni contra patriam ducere exercĭtum: si quidem licere dicimus quod legibus conceditur. 12. Non libet mihi deplorare vitam, quod multi, et ii docti sæpe fecerunt: neque me vixisse pœnĭtet, quoniam ita vixi ut non frustra me natum existĭmem. 13. Sperare videor Cæsari collēgæ nostro fore curæ ut habeamus aliquam rempublicam. 14. Fibrenum opīnor illi altĕri flumĭni nomen esse. 15. Dāturus es huic crimĭni, quod et potuisti prohibere ne (§ 45) fieret, et debuisti? 16. Cum ad me frater venisset, imprīmis nobis sermo, isque multus, de te fuit; ex quo veni ad ea, quæ fueramus ego et tu inter nos de sorōre locūti.

LESSON XV.

OTHER USES OF THE ACCUSATIVE.

§ 71. Verbs of *teaching* and *concealing* govern *two* accusatives; one of the *person*, another of the *thing*. So also does *moneo* with a *neuter pronoun*. But with all these verbs the *thing* is often in the *ablative* with *de*.

§ 72. Some verbs of *asking*, *enquiring*, and the like, also govern *two* accusatives; as "rogo, *qm. qd.*"="to ask *aby.*, *athg.*;" but "quærere *qd. ex quo*," "petere *qd. a quo.*" Instead of the accusative of the *thing*, we have very often a *sentence* preceded by "*ut*," or "*ne*," either expressed or understood, or by an interrogative.

§ 73. All the verbs which govern two accusatives in the *active*, may govern, when used personally in the *passive*, an accusative of the *thing*.

§ 74. Verbs of *clothing* are not found with *two* accusatives in the *active*; but in the *passive* some of them take an accusative of the *thing*. This is a poetical construction.

§ 75. Allied to this, and also a poetical construction, is the accusative of the *part affected*, after participles, adjectives, and sometimes intransitive verbs. This accusative is sometimes said to be governed by "*secundum*" meaning *as to* understood. Such a phrase = the active participle "*having*, &c."

§ 76. An accusative of exclamation is used after *O*, *heu*, and *proh*; and even alone.

§ 77. An *intransitive* verb may, as in English, have after it an *accusative* of a *cognate* noun.

§ 78. "Fortūna *victos* quoque belli *artem* docet"= "fortune teaches the *conquered* too the *art* of war." "Imperātor *consilium omnes* celabat"="the general concealed his *design from everybody*." "*De itinere* hostium *senatum* edŏcet"="he informs *the senate of the march* of the enemy." "*Pācem te* poscĭmus omnes"= "we all call upon *you for peace*." "Si *te* rogavero *aliquid* nonne respondebis?"="if I shall ask *you for anything*, will you not answer." "*Hoc a rege* plurĭmis verbis petit"="he begs *this of the king* with many words." "Rogo *(te) (ut) hoc facias*"="I ask you *to do* this." "Scito primum me non esse rogatum *sententiam*"="know that I was not first asked my *opiniono*." "Cingĭtur *inutile ferrum*"="he is girt *with a useless sword*." "*Ardentes oculos suffecti* sangŭine et igni"="*suffused as to their glowing eyes* with blood and fire;" i.e., "*having their glowing eyes suffused*, &c." "Heu *me miserum*"="ah *me miserable*;" "oh *acutos homines*"="oh the *clever fellows."* " *Tutiorem vitam* sese meo præsidio *victuros* arbitrantur "=" they think they will *live a safer life* under my protection."

1. Oratiōnes me duas postŭlas; quarum alteram non libebat mihi scribere, quia abscĭderam, alteram ne laudarem eum, quem non amabam.** 2. Si Deos omnes hominesque rem celare possīmus, nil injuste est faciendum. 3. A. Titurius, quum procul Ambiorĭgem suos cohortantem conspexisset, interprĕtem suum ad eum mittit, rogatum, ut sibi militibusque parcat. 4. Solon, cum interrogaretur cur nullum supplicium constituisset in eum qui parentem necasset, respondit, se id nemĭnem facturum putasse. 5. Hector redit exuvias indūtus Achillis. 6. Os humĕrosque deo simĭlis. 8. Perfūsus sanie vittas atroque venēno. 9. O misĕrum senem, qui mortem contemnendam esse in tam longa ætāte non viderit. 10. O me misĕrum! O infelīcem! revocare tu me in patriam, Mīlo, potuisti per hos: ego te in patria per eosdem retinere non potero? 11. Postulavit, ne aut Eduis, aut eorum sociis bellum inferret. 12. Rogavit milites, cur de sua virtute aut de ipsīus diligentia desperarent. 13. Mittit rogatum vasa ea, quæ pulcherrima** apud illum viderat; ait se suis cœlatoribus velle ostendere. Rex, qui istum** non nosset,** sine ulla suspiciōne libentissime dedit. 14. Adeŏne erat stultus, ut illam, quam tum ille vivebat, vitam esse arbitraretur. 15. Quæ fieri vellet, ostendit; monuitque (ut) ad nutum et ad tempus omnes res ab iis administrarentur.

LESSON XVI.

OTHER USES OF THE ABLATIVE.

§ 79. With verbs of *buying, selling, esteeming,* and *valuing,* the *price* or *cost* is put in the ablative when expressed by a *definite* sum. Of the *indefinite* price see § 65.

§ 80. The ablative without a preposition is used in some general designations of place; thus, " terra marique " =" *by* sea and land;" " secundo loco "=" *in* a favourable place."

§ 81. The ablative is the *immediate* object of the deponent verbs *fungor, fruor, utor, vescor, pascor, nitor,* (I rely on) and their compounds. But *nitor,* in *this* sense, also takes *in* with the *ablative.* " Niti *ad* or *in* qd."= " to strive *after athg.*"

§ 82. The ablative is the *immediate* object of intransitive verbs denoting *plenty* or *want,*[5] such as *abundo, careo, vaco,* &c. and of *supersedeo* when it =" *I abstain from.*" *Egeo* and *indigeo* sometimes take a *genitive* instead of the *ablative.*

§ 83. With verbs of *removing, keeping at a distance, delivering,* and others which imply *separation,* the ablative is used either *alone* or preceded by a *preposition.*

§ 84. Many verbs compounded with prepositions governing the ablative have their immediate object in that case ; thus, " *navibus* egrĕdi "=" to leave the *ships.*" Sometimes the preposition is repeated ; as, " *ex navi* egrĕdi."

§ 85. An adjective in the comparative degree, when in the nominative or accusative *with infinitive,* governs the ablative. In other cases it is generally followed by *quam,* coupling the following noun in the case of the comparative. When the comparison is between adjectives *both* may be in the comparative degree.

§ 86. " *Grandis natu* "=" *aged ;*" " *major natu* "= " *somewhat old, older, one who is older, a forefather.*" So " *minor, maximus,* &c. *natu.*"

§ 87. The impersonal *Opus est* = *there is need of,* governs a *dative* of the *person who needs,* and an *ablative* of the *thing needed ;* " Opus est *cui. quo.*"=" *aby.* has need of (wants) *athg.* But with neuters of pronouns and adjectives *opus* is often an indeclinable adjective, and = *necessary ;* " *Multa opus* sunt cui."=" *many things* are *necessary* to aby." " *Usus est* "=" there is *need of,*" is also impersonal, but is generally found without any case.

§ 88. The ablative expresses the excess or defect of one thing as compared with another. With comparatives, " *quo—eo* or *hoc,*" or " *quanto—tanto* "=" *the—the ;*" " *altero tanto*"=" *twice as much.*"

§ 89. " *Denis* in diem *assibus* anĭma[ ] et corpus milītum æstimantur "=" the life and body of a soldier are valued at *ten asses* a day." " *Multo sanguine* ea victoria iis stetit"=" the victory *cost* them *much blood.*" " Quum victoria posset *uti, frui* maluit"=" he chose to *enjoy* the victory when he might have *used* it, or, instead of *using*

it." " *Nulla re nititur* sapiens nisi *virtute"*=" a wise man
relies on nothing but *virtue."* " Docebis *carere omni malo*
mortem"=" you will show that death is *free from every
evil."* " *Indigeo tui consilii"*=" *I am in want of your
advice."* " Virtūte regis *bello liberati sunt"*=" they *were
delivered from war* by the virtue of their king." " Patria
mihi *vita mea* multo est *carior"*=" my country is much
dearer to me *than my life."* " *Tibi* ergo *opera nostra opus
est"*=" *you want* then *our assistance."* " *Quo* quid diffi-
cilius, *hoc* præclarius"=" *the* more difficult a thing is, *the*
more honourable it is."

1. Hanc vitam quiētam atque otiōsam secūti sumus ;
quæ, quoniam honōre caret, caret etiam molestia. 2.
Utuntur aut ære aut annŭlis ferreis, ad certum pondus
examinātis, pro nummo. 3. Nostri, hujus omnīno generis
pugnæ imperīti, non eādem alacritāte ac studio, quo in
pedestribus uti prœliis consueverant, utebantur. 4. Circiter millia passuum septem ab eo loco progressus, aperto
ac plano litŏre naves constituit. 5. Villam quingentis millibus, *(fundum)* sestertiis[39] ducentis quinquaginta millibus, æstimarunt.[36] 6. In Sicilia sestertiis binis tritĭci
modius erat. 7. Persuadent finitĭmis ut, eodem usi consilio, oppĭdis suis vicisque exustis, una cum iis proficis-
cantur. 8. Id est cujusque proprium, quo quisque fruitur
atque utitur. 9. Immānes et feras belluas nanciscimur
venando, ut et vescamur iis, et exerceamur in venando ad
similitudinem bellĭcæ disciplīnæ. 10. Natura fert, ut eis
faveamus, qui eādem pericŭla, quibus nos perfuncti sumus,
ingrediantur. 11. Cæsar primo, et propter multitudĭnem
hostium, et propter eximiam opiniōnem virtūtis, prœlio
supersedere statuit. 12. De media nocte Cæsar, iisdem
ducibus usus, qui nuntii venerant, sagittarios et funditōres
subsidio oppidānis mittit. 13. Apud vetĕres Germānos
quemcunque mortalium arcere tecto nefas habebatur. 14.
Quæ est in hominibus tanta perversĭtas ut, inventis fru-
gibus, glande vescantur ? 15. Parvi primo ortu sic jacent,
tanquam omnīno sine animo sint ; cum autem paullum
firmitātis accesserit, et anĭmo utuntur, et sensibus ; con-
nitunturque ut sese erĭgant, et manibus utantur ; et eos
agnoscunt a quibus educantur ; deinde æqualibus delec-
tantur, libenterque se cum his congrĕgant, dantque se ad
ludendum ; fabellarumque auditiōne ducuntur. 16. Nihil

est præclarius mundi administratiōne; Deorum igitur consilio administratur. 17. Nihil est detestabilius dedecŏre, nihil fœdius servitūte : ad decus et ad libertātem nati sumus ; aut hæc teneamus, aut cum dignitāte moriamur. 18. Nunc mihi et consiliis opus est tuis, et amōre, et fide ; quare advŏla : expedīta erunt mihi omnia, si te habebo. 19. Homines, quo plura habent, eo cupiunt ampliōra. 20. Filius altero tanto amplius habebit quam uxor. 21. Priusquam incipias consulto, ubi consulueris matūre facto, opus est.

APPENDIX I.

---

1. When either of the figures 1, 2, or 4, stands alone after a verb, it is meant that the verb is formed *exactly* like amo, moneo, or audio respectively.

2. " Nostri," " sui," &c. very often =" our, their, &c. *friends, soldiers*," &c.   So also " mea," " tua "=" my, thy, *goods, property.*"

3. An adjective in agreement with the nominative sometimes = an adverb.   Thus, " *invitus* " = " unwillingly."

4. The reciprocal pronoun *sui* and its possessive *suus* can only stand for the same person as the nominative of the sentence, which determines the *number* and *gender* of the pronoun; thus, " diligit *se* "=" he loves *himself ;*" " diligunt *se* "=" they love *themselves ;*" "misit *suos* libros " =" he (or she) sent *his* (or *her*) books ;" " miserunt *suum* librum "=" they sent *their* book."

5.   A, ab, absque, abs *and* de
Coram, clam, cum, ex *and* e
Tenus, sine, pro *and* præ
Always govern the ablative.

It is of the *utmost* importance to distinguish between " *in*" with *acc.* and " *in*" with *abl.*

6. " *Tenus* " follows its case, and with a plural noun governs the genitive, as " lumb*orum* tenus."   *Uterque* is used of two singular nouns; *utrique* when one or both are plural.

7. After verbs of *appearing, thinking,* &c. a past participle passive is sometimes used in Latin instead of an infinitive; thus, " *objectæ* existimantur "=" are thought *to lie in the way.*"

D

8. Beginners should always translate the abl. abs. *literally*, and to do so, *take the noun first.*

9. After " sinemus " supply the acc. " *them.*"

10. Whether the acc. and inf. is subject or object, is at once determined by applying the proper test ; " dicit se esse beatum ;" says *what ?* " Constat te esse beatum " *what* is evident ?

11. The " that " may in many instances be omitted, " he said (that) he was happy." Beginners however should not omit it.

12. When the *relative* is the acc. *before the inf.* it must of course = the nom. " *Quem* s. d." = " *who* as I have before pointed out, *had been sent.*"

13. When *et* is repeated the first " *et* " = " *both,*" the second = " *and.*"

14. In a simple sentence the verb cannot be in the subjunctive. What looks like the subjunctive is really the *imperative.*

15. *Ut,* " *in order that* " expresses a *purpose ; ut,* " *so that,*" introduces a *consequence,* and is preceded by a word meaning " *so* " or " such." *Ut* followed by an *indicative* = *as* or *when.*

16. After *ask, command, advise, and strive,* " ut " with the subj. almost always = the infinitive.

17. A " hypothetical proposition " consists of two simple sentences combined by the conjunction *if ;* thus, *If a were b, c would be d.*

18. A *superlative* preceded by " quam " and followed by some tense of " posse " expresses the highest possible degree ; " *quam p. p.* naves " = " *as many* ships *as possible ;* so also " *quam primum* " = " *as soon as possible.*"

19. " *Plus* posse " = " to be *more* powerful ;" " *plurimum* posse " = " to be the *most powerful ;*" so also " plus and plurimum valere.

20. " Ne *quis* " = " *that no one ;*" " ne *quid* " = " *that nothing ;*" so also " si *quis* " = " *if any,*" and " num *quis* " = " *whether any ;*" " ne quam mult. transduceret " = " that he would lead no large number."

21. Neapolis—gen. *is,* acc. *im,* abl. *i :* many proper names are thus declined.

22. " *Neque* " when standing alone frequently = " *and not.*" So here " neque quisquam " = " and nobody."

23. " *Atque* " or " *ac* " after " par," " pariter," &c. =

" *as.*" So here " pari spátio *atque*"="of an equal *(the same)* length *as.*"

24. These verbs are merely " uniting " verbs, *i.e.*, they simply affirm the indentity of the subject and predicate.

25. " *Qui*" after a word meaning " so " or " such " ="*as.*"

26. " *Ne*" interrogative, " *que*," " *ve*," cannot stand alone, but are joined to the *first* word of a clause, and are called " *enclitics*," because they throw the accent forward.

27. " Minari " or " minitari *qd. cui*"=" To threaten *aby. with athg.* :"

> " He *threatens me with death*, will be
> In Latin, *threatens death to me.*"

28. The primary meaning of " *agere*" is " *to put in motion*," " *to give an impulse to* ;" but in order to translate it regard must be had to the meaning of the accusative it governs." Thus, " agere *te*"=" to *go*," " agere *gratias*"=" to *give thanks*," " agere *vitam*"=" to *lead a life*." " *Quid agis ?*"=" *How do you do ?*" or, " *what are you doing.*" " *Quid agitur*"=" *What is going on ?*"

29. " *Non solum—sed* (or *verum*) etiam "=" not only —but also."

30. " *Quisque*" or " *unusquisque*"=" *each* or *every one* ;" " *quisquis*"=" *whosoever* ;" " *quisquam*" or " *ullus*" =" *any*, when all are *excluded* ;" " *quivis*" or " *quilibet*" =" *any*, when all are *included*, any *one* you *please* ;" " *quispiam*" or " *aliquis* "=" *some, some one or other.*"

31. " *In gratiam redire* "=" *to become friends.*"

32. " *Iste*" usually expresses *contempt* ; " *ille*," admiration.

33. " *Pro*" frequently =" *in comparison with*" or " *in proportion to.*" " *Pro cultu G.*"=" *considering the way of living among the G.*"

34. " *Alteram—alteram* "=" *the one—the other* ;" so also, " *Alius—alius.*" This sentence is an example of the epistolary style in which the Romans used the *imperfect and pluperfect*, where *we* use the *present indefinite and present perfect* ; thus, " *libebat*"=" I *do* not choose ;" " *abscideram*"=" I have torn," &c.

35. " *Necasset*" for " *necavisset.*" This omission of a syllable, which is very common in tenses derived from perfects in *vi*, is called *Syncope*. Many other words un-

dergo syncope, especially in the poets; thus, "*Deum*" for "deorum," &c.

36. An adjective very often appears in the relative clause, which must be translated with the *antecedent*. "*Vasa ea, quæ pulcherrima*"="*those very beautiful vases, which, &c.*"

37. This ablative is very near akin to the ablative of *instrument*.

38. "*Anima*"="*the breath, the vital principle, the soul apart from the body.*" "*Animus*"="*the mind with its passions and feelings, the heart, the disposition.*" "*Mens*" ="*the intellect, the reasoning faculty.*"

39. "*Sestertius*" was a coin equal to *nearly* twopence; 1,000 sestertii = £8·072916. A *sestertium* represented a *sum* not a coin.

40. "*Fert*"="*directs;*" "*Perfuncti sumus*"="*we have passed through.*"

CÆSAR'S INVASIONS OF BRITAIN.

———

CAP. 1. EXIGUA PARTE ÆSTATIS[1]* reliqua, Cæsar, etsi in his locis, quod omnis Gallia ad Septentriones vergit, maturæ sunt hiemes, tamen in Britanniam proficisci contendit, quod omnibus fere Gallicis bellis, hostibus nostris inde subministrata auxilia intelligebat; et, si tempus anni ad bellum gerendum deficeret, tamen magno sibi usui (§ 67) fore arbitrabatur, si modo insulam adisset, genus hominum perspexisset, loca, portus, aditus cognovisset; quæ omnia fere Gallis erant incognita. Neque enim temere præter mercatores illo adit quisquam; neque iis ipsis quidquam, præter oram maritimam atque eas regiones quæ sunt contra Gallias, notum est. Itaque, evocatis ad se undique mercatoribus, neque quanta esset[2] insulæ magnitudo, neque quæ aut quantæ nationes incolerent, neque quem usum belli haberent, aut quibus institutis (§ 81) uterentur, neque qui essent ad majorem navium multitudinem idonei portus, reperire poterat.

CAP. 2. Ad hæc cognoscenda, prius quam periculum faceret, idoneum esse arbitratus C. Volusenum cum navi longa[3] præmittit. Huic mandat, uti, exploratis omnibus rebus, ad se quam primum[4] revertatur: ipse cum omnibus copiis in Morinos proficiscitur, quod inde erat brevissimus in Britanniam transjectus. Huc naves undique ex finitimis regionibus, et, quam superiore æstate fecerat, classem jubet convenire. Interim, consilio ejus cognito et per mercatores perlato ad Britannos, a compluribus ejus insulæ civitatibus ad eum legati veniunt, qui polliceantur (§ 44) obsides dare,[5] atque imperio Populi Romani obtemperare,

---

* These numbers refer to Appendix II. which follows.

Quibus⁶ auditis, liberalitur pollicitus, hortatusque ut in ea sententia permanerent, eos domum remittit; et cum his una Commium, quem sibi fidelem arbitrabatur, cujusque auctoritas in iis regionibus magni (§ 65) habebatur, mittit. Huic imperat, quas possit, adeat civitates, horteturque ut Populi Romani fidem sequantur;⁷ seque celeriter eo venturum nuntiet. Volusenus, perspectis regionibus, quinto die ad Cæsarem revertitur; quæque ibi perspexisset, renuntiat.

Cap. 3. Navibus circiter LXXX onerariis coactis quot satis esse ad duas transportandas legiones⁸ existimabat; quidquid præterea navium longarum habebat, quæstori, legatis, præfectisque distribuit. Huc accedebant XVIII onerariæ naves, quæ ex eo loco ab millibus passuum VIII vento tenebantur, quominus (§ 45) in eundem portum pervenire possent. Has equitibus distribuit. P. Sulpicium Rufum, legatum, cum eo præsidio quod satis esse arbitrabatur, portum tenere jussit.

Cap. 4. His constitutis⁹ rebus, nactus idoneam ad navigandum tempestatem, tertia fere vigilia¹⁰ solvit, equitesque in ulteriorem portum progredi, et naves conscendere, et se sequi jussit: a quibus¹¹ quum id paulo tardius esset administratum, ipse hora diei circiter quarta¹² cum primis navibus Britanniam attigit, atque ibi in omnibus collibus expositas hostium copias armatas conspexit. Cujus loci hæc erat natura: adeo montibus angustis mare continebatur, uti ex locis superioribus in litus telum adjici posset. Hunc ad egrediendum nequaquam idoneum arbitratus locum, dum reliquæ naves eo convenirent, ad horam nonam, in anchoris exspectavit. Interim legatis tribunisque militum convocatis, et quæ ex Voluseno cognovisset, et quæ fieri vellet, ostendit, monuitque (ut) ad nutum et ad tempus omnes res ab iis administrarentur. His dimissis, et ventum et æstum uno tempore nactus secundum, dato signo et sublatis anchoris, circiter millia passuum VII ab eo loco progressus, aperto ac plano litore naves constituit.

Cap. 5. At barbari, consilio Romanorum cognito, præmisso equitatu et essedariis, quo plerumque genere¹³ in prœliis uti consuerunt, reliquis copiis subsecuti, nostros navibus egredi prohibebant. Erat ob has causas summa difficultas, quod naves, propter magnitudinem, nisi in alto¹⁴

constitui non poterant; militibus (§ 33) autem,[15] ignotis
locis, impeditis manibus, magno et gravi armorum onere
oppressis,[16] simul et de navibus desiliendum, et in flucti-
bus consistendum, et cum hostibus erat pugnandum; quum
illi aut ex arido, aut paululum in aquam progressi, omni
bus membris expediti, notissimis locis, audacter tela conji-
cerent, et equos insuefactos[17] incitarent. Quibus[18] rebus[17] nostri perterriti, atque hujus omnino generis pugnæ
imperiti, non eadem alacritate ac studio, quo in pedestribus
uti prœliis consueverant, utebantur.

CAP. 6. Quod[19] ubi Cæsar animum advertit, naves
longas, quarum species erat barbaris inusitatior, paulum
removeri ab onerariis navibus, et remis incitari, et ad[20]
latus apertum hostium constitui, atque inde fundis, sagittis,
tormentis, hostes submoveri jussit; quæ res magno usui
nostris fuit. Nam, et navium figura, et remorum motu, et
inusitato genere tormentorum permoti, barbari constiterunt,
ac paulum modo pedem[21] retulerunt. Atque nostris
militibus cunctantibus, maxime propter altitudinem maris,
qui decimæ legionis aquilam ferebat,[22] contestatus deos,
ut ea res[23] legioni feliciter eveniret : " Desilite," inquit,
" commilitones, nisi vultis aquilam hostibus prodere ; ego
" certe meum reipublicæ atque imperatori officium præ-
" sitero." Hoc quum magna voce dixisset, ex navi se
projecit, atque in hostes aquilam ferre cœpit. Tum nostri, cohortati inter se[24] ne tantum dedecus admitteretur,
universi ex navi desiluerunt.

CAP. 7. Pugnatum est ab utrisque acriter. Nostri tamen, quod neque ordines servare, neque firmiter insistere,
neque signa subsequi poterant, atque alius[25] alia ex navi,
quibuscumque signis occurrerat, se aggregabat, magnopere
perturbabantur. Hostes vero, notis omnibus vadis, ubi
ex litore aliquos singulares ex navi egredientes conspexerant, incitatis equis impeditos adoriebantur; plures pau-
cos circumsistebant; alii ab[26] latere aperto in universos
tela conjiciebant. Quod quum animum advertisset[19] Cæsar, scaphas longarum navium, item speculatoria navigia
militibus compleri jussit, et, quos laborantes conspexerat,
iis subsidia submittebat. Nostri, simul[27] in arido constiterunt, in hostes impetum fecerunt, atque eos in fugam
dederunt neque longius[28] prosequi potuerunt, quod equites

cursum tenere[29] atque insulam capere non potuerant. Hoc unum ad pristinam fortunam Cæsari defuit.

CAP. 8. Hostes prœlio superati, simul atque se ex fuga receperunt, statim ad Cæsarem legatos de pace miserunt: obsides daturos, quæque imperasset sese facturos, polliciti sunt. Una cum his legatis Commius venit, quem supra demonstraveram[30] a Cæsare in Britanniam præmissum. Hunc illi e navi egressum, quum ad eos imperatoris mandata perferret, comprehenderant atque in vincula conjecerant: tum prœlio facto, remiserunt, et in petenda pace ejus rei culpam in multitudinem contulerunt, et, propter imprudentiam, ut ignosceretur (§ 24) petiverunt. Cæsar questus, quod, quum ultro in continentem legatis missis pacem ab se petissent, bellum sine causa intulissent, ignoscere imprudentiæ dixit, obsidesque imperavit; quorum illi partem statim dederunt, partem, ex longinquioribus locis arcessitam[31] paucis diebus sese daturos dixerunt. Interea suos remigrare in agros jusserunt; principesque undique convenire et se civitatesque suas Cæsari commendare cœperunt.

CAP. 9. His rebus pace confirmata, post[32] diem quartum quam est in Britanniam ventum,[33] naves, quæ equites sustulerant, ex superiore portu leni vento solverunt.[10] Quæ[34] quum appropinquarent Britanniæ, et ex castris viderentur, tanta tempestas subito coorta est, ut nulla earum cursum tenere posset; sed aliæ eodem, unde erant profectæ, referrentur; aliæ ad inferiorem partem insulæ, quæ est propius solis occasum, magno sui[35] cum periculo dejicerentur: quæ tamen, continentem[36] petierunt.

CAP. 10. Eadem nocte accidit,[37] ut esset luna plena, qui dies[38] maritimos æstus maximos in Oceano efficere consuevit; nostrisque id erat incognitum. Ita uno tempore, et longas naves, quas in aridum subduxerat, æstus complebat, et onerarias, quæ ad anchoras erant deligatæ, tempestas afflictabat; neque ulla nostris facultas auxiliandi, dabatur. Compluribus navibus fractis, reliquæ quum essent, funibus, anchoris, reliquisque armamentis amissis, ad navigandum inutiles, magna, id quod (§ 36) necesse erat accidere, totius exercitus perturbatio facta est: neque enim naves erant aliæ, quibus reportari, possent; et omnia

deerant, quæ ad reficiendas eas usui sunt; et, quod omnibus constabat hiemare in Gallia oportere, frumentum his
in locis in (§ 48) hiemem provisum non erat.

CAP. 11. Quibus rebus cognitis, principes Britanniæ,
qui post prœlium factum[39] ad ea, quæ jusserat Cæsar,
facienda convenerant, inter se[40] collocuti, optimum factu
(§ 29) esse duxerunt, rebellione facta, frumento commea-
tuque nostros prohibere, et rem[41] in hiemem producere;
quod, iis superatis, aut reditu interclusis, neminem, postea
belli inferendi causa in Britanniam transiturum confidebant.
Itaque paulatim ex castris discedere, ac suos clam ex agris
deducere cœperunt.

CAP. 12. At Cæsar, etsi nondum eorum consilia cognoverat,[42] tamen et ex eventu navium suarum, et ex eo,
quod obsides dare intermiserant, fore id, quod accidit,[43]
suspicabatur. Itaque ad omnes casus subsidia comparabat:
nam et frumentum ex agris quotidie in castra conferebat;
et, quæ gravissime afflictæ erant naves, earum (§38) materia
atque ære ad reliquas reficiendas utebatur; et, quæ ad eas
res erant usui (§ 67) ex continenti comportari jubebat.
Itaque, quum id summo studio a militibus administraretur,
XII. navibus amissis, reliquis ut navigari[44] commode
posset, effecit.

CAP. 13. Dum ea geruntur, legione ex consuetudine una
frumentatum (§ 29) missa, quæ appellabatur septima, neque
ulla ad id tempus belli suspicione interposita, quum pars
hominum in agris remaneret, pars etiam in castra ventitaret,[45] ii, qui pro portis castrorum in statione[46] erant,
Cæsari renuntiaverunt, pulverem majorem, quam con-
suetudo ferret, in ea parte[47] videri, quam in partem (§ 37)
legio iter fecisset. Cæsar, suspicatus, aliquid novi a
barbaris initum consilii (§ 13) cohortes, quæ in stationibus
erant, secum in eam partem proficisci, duas ex reliquis in
stationem succedere, reliquas armari et confestim sese
subsequi jussit. Quum paulo longius a castris processisset,
suos ab hostibus premi, atque ægre sustinere, et conferta
legione ex omnibus partibus tela conjici, animadvertit.
Nam quod, omni ex reliquis partibus demesso frumento,
pars una erat reliqua, suspicati hostes, huc nostros esse
venturos, noctu in silvis delituerant; tum dispersos,[48]

depositis armis, in metendo occupatos subito adorti, paucis
interfectis, reliquos incertis ordinibus perturbaverant;
simul²⁷ equitatu atque essedis circumdederant.

CAP. 14. " Genus hoc est ex essedis pugnæ: primo per
omnes partes perequitant, et tela conjiciunt, atque ipso⁴⁹
terrore equorum, et strepitu rotarum, ordines plerumque
perturbant; et, quum se inter equitum turmas⁴⁹* insi-
nuaverint, ex essedis desiliunt et pedibus prœliantur.
Aurigæ⁵⁰ interim paulatim ex prœlio excedunt, atque ita
currus collocant, ut, si illi⁵⁰ a multitudine hostium pre-
mantur, expeditum⁵¹ ad suos receptum habeant. Ita
mobilitatem equitum, stabilitatem peditum, in prœliis
præstant, ac tantum usu quotidiano et exercitatione effi-
ciunt, uti, in declivi ac præcipiti loco,⁵² incitatos equos
sustinere, et brevi moderari ac flectere, et per temonem
percurere, et in jugo insistere, et inde se in currus citissime
recipere consuerint."

CAP. 15. Perturbatis nostris novitate pugnæ, tempore
opportunissimo Cæsar auxilium tulit: namque ejus ad-
ventu hostes constiterunt, nostri se ex timore receperunt.
Quo facto, ad lacessendum et ad committendum⁵⁴ prœlium
alienum esse tempus arbitratus, suo se loco continuit, et,
brevi tempore intermisso, in castra legiones reduxit. Dum
hæc⁵⁵ geruntur, nostris omnibus occupatis, qui erant in
agris, discesserunt. Secutæ sunt continuos complures dies
(§ 48) tempestates, quæ⁵⁶ et nostros in castris continerent,
et hostem a pugna prohiberent. Interim barbari nuntios in
omnes partes dimiserunt, paucitatemque nostrorum militum suis prædicaverunt,⁵⁷ et, quanta prædæ faciendæ, atque
in perpetuum⁵⁸ sui liberandi, facultas daretur, si Romanos
castris expulissent, demonstraverunt. His rebus celeriter
magna multitudine peditatus equitatusque coacta, ad
castra venerunt.

CAP. 16. Cæsar, etsi idem, quod superioribus diebus
acciderat, fore videbat, ut, si essent hostes pulsi, celeritate
periculum effugerent; tamen nactus equites circiter xxx,
quos Commius, de quo ante dictum est, secum trans-
portaverat, legiones in acie pro castris constituit. Commisso prœlio, diutius nostrorum militum impetum hostes
ferre non potuerunt, ac terga verterunt. Quos⁶ tanto⁵⁹

spatio secuti, quantum cursu efficere potuerunt, complures ex iis occiderunt;[60] deinde omnibus longe lateque afflictis incensisque, se in castra receperunt.

CAP. 17. Eodem die legati, ab hostibus missi, ad Cæsarem de pace venerunt. His[61] Cæsar numerum obsidum, quem antea imperaverat, duplicavit, eosque in continentem adduci jussit; quod, propinqua die æquinoctii,[62] infirmis navibus, hiemi navigationem subjiciendam non existimabat. Ipse, idoneam tempestatem nactus, paulo post mediam noctem naves solvit, quæ omnes incolumes ad continentem pervenerunt; sed ex his onerariæ duæ eosdem, quos[63] reliquæ, portus capere[64] non potuerunt et paulo infra delatæ sunt. Duæ omnino civitates ex Britannia obsides miserunt, reliquæ neglexerunt. His rebus gestis, ex literis Cæsaris[64] dierum xx supplicatio a senatu decreta est.

CAP. 18. PROXIMO ANNO,[65] cum v legionibus et duobus millibus equitum solis occasu naves solvit; et, leni Africo provectus, media circiter nocte vento intermisso, cursum non tenuit; et, longius delatus æstu, orta luce, sub sinistra Britanniam relictam conspexit. Tum rursus, æstus commutationem secutus, remis contendit, ut eam partem insulæ caperet, qua optimum esse egressum superiore æstate cognoverat. Qua in re admodum fuit militum virtus laudanda, qui vectoriis gravibusque navigiis, non intermisso remigandi labore, longarum navium cursum adequarunt. Accessum est ad Britanniam omnibus navibus meridiano fere tempore : neque in eo loco hostis est visus, sed, ut postea Cæsar ex captivis comperit, quum magnæ manus eo convenissent, multitudine navium perterritæ a litore discesserant ac se in superiora loca abdiderant.

CAP. 19. Cæsar, exposito exercitu et loco castris idoneo capto, ubi ex captivis cognovit, quo in loco hostium copiæ consedissent, cohortibus x ad mare relictis et equitibus ccc, qui præsidio navibus essent, de tertia vigilia ad hostes contendit, eo (§ 88) minus veritus navibus, quod in litore molli atque aperto deligatas ad anchoram relinquebat; et præsidio navibus Q. Atrium præfecit. Ipse, noctu progressus millia passuum circiter xii. hostium copias conspicatus est. Illi, equitatu atque essedis ad flumen progressi, ex loco superiore nostros prohibere et proelium committere coeperunt. Repulsi ab equitatu, se in silvas abdiderunt, locum nacti, egregie et natura, et opere munitum, quem domestici belli, ut videbatur, causa jam ante praeparaverant : nam crebris[66] arboribus succisis omnes introitus erant praeclusi. Ipsi ex silvis rari propugnabant, nostrosque intra munitiones ingredi prohibebant. At milites legionis septimae, testudine facta[67] et aggere ad munitiones adjecto, locum ceperunt eosque ex silvis expulerunt, paucis vulneribus acceptis. Sed eos fugientes longius Caesar prosequi vetuit, et quod loci naturam ignorabat, et quod, magna parte diei consumpta, munitioni castrorum tempus relinqui volebat.

Cap. 20. Postridie ejus diei mane tripartito milites[68] equitesque in expeditionem misit, ut eos, qui fugerant, persequerentur. His aliquantum itineris progressis, quum jam extremi[69] essent in prospectu, equites a Q. Atrio ad Caesarem venerunt, qui nuntiarent, superiore nocte, maxima coorta tempestate, prope omnes naves afflictas atque in litore ejectas esse; quod neque anchorae funesque subsisterent,[70] neque nautae gubernatoresque vim pati tempestatis possent : itaque ex eo concursu navium magnum esse incommodum acceptum.

Cap. 21. His rebus cognitis, Caesar legiones equitatumque revocari atque itinere desistere jubet; ipse ad naves revertitur : eadem fere, quae[71] ex nuntiis literisque cognoverat coram perspicit, sic ut, amissis circiter XL navibus, reliquae tamen refici posse magno negotio viderentur. Itaque ex legionibus fabros deligit, et ex continenti alios arcessiri jubet; Labieno scribit, ut quam plurimas posset[72] iis legionibus quae sunt apud eum, naves instituat. Ipse, etsi res erat multae operae ac laboris, tamen commodissimum esse statuit, omnes naves subduci et cum castris una munitione conjungi. In his rebus circiter dies consumit, ne nocturnis quidem temporibus ad laborem militum intermissis. Subductis navibus castrisque egregie munitis, easdem copias, quas ante, praesidio (§ 67) navibus reliquit; ipse eodem, unde redierat, proficiscitur. Eo quum venisset, majores jam undique in eum locum copiae Britannorum convenerant; summa[73] imperii bellique administrandi, communi consilio, permissa Cassivellauno, cujus fines a

maritimis civitatibus flumen dividit, quod appellatur
Tamesis, a mari circiter millia passuum LXXX.[74]

CAP. 22. " Britanniæ pars interior ab iis incolitur, quos
natos (§ 34) in insula ipsa, dicunt; maritima pars ab iis,
qui prædæ ac belli inferendi causa ex Belgis transierant,
et bello illato ibi remanserunt atque agros colere cœperunt.
Hominum est infinita multitudo, creberrimaque ædificia
fere Gallicis consimilia; pecorum magnus numerus. Utuntur aut ære, aut taleis[75] ferreis ad certum pondus ex-
aminatis, pro nummo. Nascitur ibi plumbum album in
mediterraneis regionibus, in maritimis ferrum;[76] sed ejus
exigua est copia : ære utuntur importato. Materia cujusque generis, ut in Gallia, est, præter fagum atque abietem.
Leporem et gallinam et anserem gustare, fas non putant;
hæc tamen aluut animi[77] voluptatisque causa. Loca sunt
temperatiora, quam in Gallia, remissioribus[78] frigoribus."

CAP. 23. [79]" Insula natura triquetra, cujus unum latus
est contra Galliam. Hujus lateris alter angulus, qui est
ad Cantium, quo fere omnes ex Gallia naves appelluntur,
ad orientem solem; inferior ad Meridiem spectat. Hoc
latus tenet circiter millia passuum D. Alterum vergit ad
Hispaniam atque occidentem solem; qua ex parte est
Hibernia[80] dimidio minor, ut æstimatur, quam Britannia;
sed pari spatio transmissus,[81] atque ex Gallia, est in
Britanniam. In hoc medio cursu est insula, quæ appellatur
Mona;[82] complures præterea minores objectæ insulæ existimantur; de quibus insulis nonnulli scripserunt, dies
continuos XXX sub bruma esse noctem. Nos nihil de
eo percontationibus reperiebamus, nisi certis ex aqua
mensuris[83] breviores esse, quam in continente, noctes videbamus. Hujus est longitudo lateris, ut fert illorum opinio,
DCC millium. Tertium est contra septentriones, cui parti
nulla est objecta terra; sed ejus angulus lateris maxime
ad Germaniam spectat: huic millia passuum DCCC in
longitudinem esse, existimatur.[84] Ita omnis insula est in
circuitu vicies centum millium passuum."

CAP. 24. " Ex his[85] omnibus longe sunt humanissimi,
qui Cantium incolunt, quæ regio est maritima omnis;
neque multum a Gallica differunt consuetudine. Interiores
plerique frumenta non serunt, sed lacte et carne vivunt,

E

pellibusque sunt vestiti. Omnes vero se Britanni vitro
inficiunt, quod cœruleum efficit colorem, atque hoc[86]
horridiore sunt in pugna aspectu (§ 18); capilloque sunt
promisso atque omni parte corporis rasa, præter caput et
labrum superius."

CAP. 25. Equites hostium essedariique acriter prœlio
cum equitatu nostro in itinere conflixerunt; tamen ut[87]
nostri omnibus partibus superiores fuerint, atque eos in
silvas collesque compulerint : sed compluribus interfectis,
cupidius insecuti, nonnullos ex suis amiserunt. At illi,
intermisso spatio, imprudentibus nostris atque occupatis in
munitione castrorum, subito se ex silvis ejecerunt, im-
petuque in eos facto, qui erant in statione pro castris
collocati, acriter pugnaverunt : duabusque missis subsidio
cohortibus a Cæsare, atque his primis[88] legionum duarum,
per medios audacissime perruperunt, seque inde incolumes
receperunt. Eo die Q. Laberius Durus, tribunus militum[8]
interficitur. Illi, pluribus immissis cohortibus repelluntur.

CAP. 26. Toto hoc in genere pugnæ, quum sub oculis
omnium ac pro castris dimicaretur, intellectum est, nostros
propter gravitatem armaturæ, quod neque insequi cedentes
possent, neque ab signis discedere auderent, minus aptos
esse ad hujus generis hostem; equites autem magno cum
periculo dimicare, propterea quod illi[89] etiam consulto
plerumque cederent, et, quum paulum ab legionibus
nostros removissent, ex essedis desilirent et pedibus
dispari prœlio contenderent. Accedebat[90] huc, ut nunquam conferti, sed rari magnisque intervallis prœliarentur,
stationesque dispositas haberent, atque alios alii deinceps
exciperent, integrique et recentes defatigatis succederent.

CAP. 27. Postero die procul a castris hostes in collibus
constiterunt, rarique se ostendere, et lenius quam pridie
nostros equites prœlio lacessere, cœperunt. Sed meridie,
quum Cæsar pabulandi causa tres legiones atque omnem
equitatum cum C. Trebonio legato misisset, repente ex
omnibus partibus ad pabulatores advolaverunt; sic, uti ab
signis legionibusque non absisterent. Nostri, acriter in
eos impetu facto, repulerunt, neque finem sequendi
fecerunt, quoad subsidio confisi[91] equites, quum post se
legiones viderent, præcipites hostes egerunt; magnoque

eorum numero interfecto, neque sui colligendi, neque consistendi, aut ex essedis desiliendi, facultatem dederunt. Ex hac fuga protinus, quæ undique convenerant, auxilia discesserunt : neque post id tempus unquam summis[92] nobiscum copiis hostes contenderunt.

CAP. 28. Cæsar, cognito consilio eorum, ad flumen Tamesin in fines Cassivellauni exercitum duxit ; quod flumen uno omnino loco pedibus, atque hoc ægre, transiri potest. Eo quum venisset, animadvertit, ad alteram fluminis ripam magnas esse copias hostium instructas ; ripa autem erat acutis sudibus præfixis[93] munita, ejusdemque generis sub aqua defixæ sudes flumine tegebantur. His rebus cognitis a captivis perfugisque, Cæsar, præmisso equitatu, confestim legiones subsequi jussit. Sed ea celeritate atque eo impetu, milites ierunt, quum capite solo ex aqua exstarent, ut hostes impetum legionum atque equitum sustinere non possent, ripasque dimitterent ac se fugæ mandarent.

CAP. 29. Cassivellaunus, ut supra demonstravimus, omni deposita spe contentionis,[95] dimissis amplioribus copiis, millibus circiter IV essedariorum relictis, itinera nostra servabat, paululumque ex via excedebat, locisque impeditis ac silvestribus sese occultabat, atque iis regionibus, quibus nos iter facturos cognoverat, pecora atque homines ex agris in silvas compellebat : et, quum equitatus noster, liberius prædandi vastandique causa, se in agros effunderet, omnibus viis notis semitisque essedarios ex silvis emittebat, et, magno cum periculo nostrorum equitum (§ 11) eum iis confligebat, atque hoc metu latius vagari prohibebat. Relinquebatur, ut neque longius ab agmine[96] legionum discedi (§ 24) Cæsar pateretur, et tantum in agris vastandis incendiisque faciendis hostibus noceretur,[97] quantum labore atque itinere legionarii milites efficere poterant.

CAP. 30. Interim Trinobantes, prope firmissima earum regionum civitas, ex qua Mandubratius adolescens, Cæsaris fidem secutus, ad eum in continentem Galliam venerat (cujus pater in ea civitate regnum obtinuerat, interfectusque erat a Cassivellauno,) legatos ad Cæsarem mittunt, pollicenturque sese ei dedituros atque imperata

facturos : petunt, ut Mandubratium ab injuria Cassivellauni (§ 11) defendat, atque in civitatem mittat, qui
(§ 44) præsit imperiumque obtineat. His Cæsar imperat
obsides XL frumentumque exercitui ; Mandubratiumque
ad eos mittit. Illi imperata celeriter fecerunt, obsides ad
numerum frumentaque miserunt.

CAP. 31. Trinobantibus defensis atque ab omni militum
injuria prohibitis, Cenimagni, aliique, legationibus missis,
sese Cæsari dedunt. Ab his cognoscit, non longe ex eo
loco oppidum Cassivellauni abesse, silvis paludibusque
munitum, quo satis magnus hominum pecorisque numerus
convenerit. " Oppidum autem Britanni vocant, quum silvas
impeditas vallo^{' '} atque fossa munierunt, quo incursionis
hostium vitandæ causa convenire consuerunt." Eo proficiscitur cum legionibus : locum reperit egregie natura
atque opere munitum ; tamen hunc duabus ex partibus
oppugnare contendit. Hostes, paulisper morati, militum
nostrorum impetum non tulerunt, seseque alia ex parte
oppidi ejecerunt. Magnus ibi numerus pecoris repertus,
multique in fuga sunt comprehensi atque interfecti.

CAP. 32. Dum hæc in his locis geruntur, Cassivellaunus
ad Cantium, quod esse ad mare supra demonstravimus,
quibus regionibus IV reges præerant, nuntios mittit, atque
his imperat, uti, coactis omnibus copiis, castra navalia de
improviso adoriantur atque oppugnent. Ii quum ad castra
venissent, nostri, eruptione facta, multis eorum interfectis,
capto etiam nobili duce, suos incolumes reduxerunt. Cassivellaunus, hoc prœlio nuntiato, tot detrimentis acceptis,
vastatis finibus, maxime etiam permotus defectione civi-
tatum, legatos per Commium de deditione ad Cæsarem
mittit. Cæsar, quum statuisset hiemem in continenti
propter repentinos Galliæ motus agere, neque multum
æstatis superesset, atque id facile extrahi posse intelligeret,
obsides imperat, et, quid in annos singulos vectigalis (§ 13)
Populo Romano Britannia penderet, constituit : imperat
Cassivellauno, ne Mandubratio, neu Trinobantibus bellum
faciat.

CAP. 33. Obsidibus acceptis, exercitum reducit ad mare,
naves invenit refectas. His deductis, quod et captivorum
magnum numerum habebat, et nonnullæ tempestate de-

perierant naves, duobus commeatibus exercitum reportare instituit. Ac sic accidit, uti ex tanto navium numero, tot navigationibus, neque hoc, neque superiore anno, ulla omnino navis, quæ milites portaret, desideraretur; at ex iis, quæ inanes ex continenti ad eum remitterentur, prioris commeatus expositis militibus, et quas postea Labienus faciendas curaverat numero LX, perpaucæ locum caperent, reliquæ fere omnes rejicerentur. Quas quum aliquamdiu Cæsar frustra expectasset, necessario angustius milites collocavit; ac secunda inita quum solvisset vigilia, prima luce terram attigit, omnesque incolumes naves perduxit.

APPENDIX II.

———

1. " *Æstatis.*" This was B.C. 55. 2. " *Esset.*" This and the following verbs are in the *subjunctive* = *the English indicative*, as dependent questions, " objects " of *reperire.* 3. " *Navis longa* "=" a *ship* of *war.*" 4. (See App. I., *note* 18.) 5. " *Dare.*" This would regularly be *se daturos* (see § 41). 6. " *Quibus.*" It is often desirable to resolve a relative into a *conjunction* and *demonstrative ;* thus, *qui* = and, now, but, &c. *he* or *they.* Here too in order to avoid changing the nominative of the sentence, " *auditis* " may be translated actively, and the whole passage = " *whereupon having given them a hearing, made them liberal promises and exhorted them,*" &c. 7. " *Ut fidem P.R. sequantur* "=" *to continue faithful to the* R.P.*" 8. " *Legiones.*" A legion contained ten *cohorts ;* a cohort, three *maniples,* and a maniple, two *centuries.* A century did not necessarily contain one hundred men. Each century was commanded by a *centurion.* The centurion of the first century of the first maniple of the first cohort was the highest in rank, and was called *Primus pilus,* or *primopilus.* He bore the eagle of the legion, and took his place in the council of war. In each legion there were six " *tribuni militum,*" who commanded in turn, usually for a month. In battle each tribune of the soldiers seems to have commanded ten centuries. The " *legati* " acted as " generals of divisions," immediately under the consul, and varied in number according to circumstances. 9. " *Constitutis.*" *Statuo* = I *cause to stand,* is the transitive of *sto* or *sisto* = I *stand.* So *constituo* and *consisto ;* con (*i.e.,* cum) having its usual force of *connection.* 10. " *Vigilia solvit.*" The Romans divided the night into four watches, beginning at six P.M. Hence

" *tertia vigilia* " lasted from midnight to three A.M. After
" *solvit* " is to be understood *naves*. " *Solvere naves* "=
" to *loosen (i.e., unmoor)* the ships or to *set sail*." 11. The
Roman cavalry was chiefly furnished by conquered nations.
The " *Equites* " here mentioned were probably Gauls:
hence their tardiness. 12. Ten o'clock A.M.

13. " *Quo—genere* "=" *which kind* of troops." 14.
" *Alto*." *Altus* means at a distance from the earth's sur-
face, either *above* or *below* it, and therefore = *high* or *deep*.
So also *profundus*. 15. " *Autem* " frequently introduces
an additional circumstance, and = *besides*, or *too*. 16.
" *Oppressis* "=" themselves *weighed down*," &c. 17.
" *Insuefactos* "=" which were *accustomed* to it." 18.
" *Quibus*," &c. *Hæc* or *ea res* often = simply *this*; so *quæ
res* = *which*. Here " *quibus rebus* "=" *by this* " (see
note 6 above).

19. " *Quod*," &c.=" *which* when Cæsar *observes*." Quod
is *acc.* gov. by the *ad.* in the verb, which is frequently
written *animadvertere*. 20. " *Ad latus apertum* "=" *a-
gainst* the unprotected flank." 21. " *Pedem referre* "=" to
retire." 22. (See *note* 8 above.) 23. (See *note* 18 above.)
24. " *Ne tantum*," &c.=" *that* such a disgrace should *not*
be suffered;" but better actively = *not to suffer*, &c.

25. " *Alius ex a. n.*"=" *one* out of *one* ship, *another*
out of *another*." 26. " *Ab latere* "=" *on* the," &c. *A*
or *ab* often signifies *on* in the sense of relative position;
so *a tergo* = *in* or *on* the rear. 27. " *Simul*." *Atque* or
ac is often understood after *simul*, and the phrase = *as
soon as*. 28. " *Longius* "= *very far*, in a *limiting* sense.
When no direct comparison is made this is often the
meaning of the comparative. 29. " *Cursum tenere* "=
" to *make* the passage." " *Capere* "=" to *reach*." 30.
" *Demonstraveram*." Here and in one or two other instances Cæsar writes in the *first* person; only, however,
in his capacity of author. 31. " *Arcessitam* "=" they
would send for *and* see " (§ 35). 32. " *Post—quam* "=
" after *adv*." is often written separately. 33. " Est ventum "=" *they* (indefinite) came." 34. " *Quæ quum* "=
" *but* when *these* " (see *note* 6 above). 35. " *Sui* "=" *to*
themselves " (see § 11). 36. " *Continentem* " (terram *understood*)=" the *continent*."

37. " *Accidit* "= *it happened*, is followed by *ut* with
subj. So also *evenit*. 38. " *Qui dies* "=" which *season*."

39. "*Post pr. fac.*"="after the battle *was over.*" 40. "*Inter se*"="with one another," sometimes "*from* one another." 41. "*Rem producere*"="to *lengthen out* the business."

42. "*Nondum cognoverat*"="he *did* not yet *know.*" "*Cognosco*"="I *become* acquainted with;" "*cognovi*"= "I *have become* acquainted with" *(i.e.*, I *know).* 43. "*Fore id. qd. accidit*"="that *that* would take place which *did* happen." 44. "*Navigari posset*"="that *it* could *be sailed*" but (see *note* 24 above). 45. "*Ventitaret*"="were *coming to and fro.*" *Frequentative* verbs denote a repetition of the act expressed by the primitive, as from *rogo*=I ask, comes *rogito*=I ask *again* and *again;* from *ago*=I put in motion, *agito*=I shake. So from *venio*, comes *ventito.* Sometimes the frequentative is used *instead of* the primitive, as "*agitare* (for *agere*) vitam"= "to lead a life." 46. "*In statione*"="*on guard.*" 47. "*In ea parte*"="in that *direction.*" 48. "*Dispersos,*" understand *nostros.*

49. "*Ipso terrore*"="by the *very* terror." 49.* In the Roman cavalry a "*turma*" consisted of three *decuriæ* or tens: and ten *turmæ, i.e.,* three hundred men constituted the *justus equitatus* or *ala* of a legion. 50. "*Aurigæ—illi.*" The chariot contained the driver, *auriga*, and the fighter, *essedarius. Illi* refers to the latter. 51. "*Expeditum receptum*"="a ready retreat." 52. "*In d. ac p. loco*"="on a steep descent." 53. "*Moderari* et *flectere*"="*check* and *turn* them." 54. "*Committ. p.*"= "to *join* battle." 55. "*Dum hæc ger.*"="while this *is* going on." 56. "*Quæ*"="of *such a kind as to,*" or, *so violent as to.* 57. "*Prædicare*"="to say *publicly,* to proclaim;" "*prædicere*"="to say *beforehand,* to foretell." 58. "*In perpetuum*"="for ever." 59. "*Tanto spatio quantum*"="as far as." 60. What is the difference between *occidere* and *occĭdere?* 61. "*His Cæsar—duplicavit*"="from these Cæsar *required twice as many hostages* as he had before demanded." 62. The Autumnal equinox. When is this? Why is it so called? 63. "*Quos.*" (See *note* 25, App. I.) 64. (See *note* 29 above.) 64. "*Ex lit. Cæsaris*"="*on the receipt of Cæsar's despatch.*"

65. This was B.C. 54. 66. "*Crebris arb. succ*"="*with felled trees stacked close together.*" 67. "*Testudine f.*" ="having formed a *testudo.*" This was a body of men

protected from the missiles of the besieged by interlocking their shields, which thus resembled the scales of a tortoise *(testudo)*. 68. "*Milites equitesque*"="*foot* and *horse* soldiers." *Milites* used emphatically always means the foot soldiers of the legion. 69. "*Extremi in prospectu*" ="almost out of sight." 70. "*Subsisterent—possent.*" These subjunctives denote the words of the messengers. The indicative would imply the words of the historian.

71. "*Eadem fere, quæ*"="almost *the same as.*" 72. "*Quam p. p.*" (See *note* 18, App. I.) 73. "*Summa imp. bell. adm.*"="the *chief command* and *direction* of the war." *Summa* is here a noun, meaning *whole* or *total,* but is used as *plus* is, in the phrase "*plus boni*" (See § 13). 74. This seems to mean from the place where Cæsar landed to the point where he crossed the river. 75. "*Annulis*"="*rings*" occurs in some editions instead of *taleis.* 76. Cæsar's description is based upon what he was told, and is inaccurate in this instance as well as in others. 77. "*Animi*"="of amusement." 78. "*Remissioribus*" (*i.e.,* slacker)="*less intense.*"

79. It is useless to attempt to make this description coincide with the true geography of Britain. Cæsar's notion of the island is a scalene triangle, with its longest side to the north. 80. So Tacitus (Agric. 24) "*Hibernia, medio inter Britanniam atque Hispaniam sita.*" 81. "*Transmissus*"="the passage." "*Pari,*" &c. (See *note* 23, App. I.) 82. "*Mona*" here means "*Man,*" elsewhere it means "*Anglesea.*" 83. "*Certis ex a. m.*"= "*accurate* water measures." 84. Observe the three different modes of expressing length. 85. "*His* Britannis." 86. "*Hoc*"="for *this* reason."

87. "*Ut*" answers to *ita,* understood with *conflixerunt.* 88. The first cohort was the most highly esteemed (see *note* 8 above). 89. "*Illi*" the Britons. 90. "*Accedebat huc, ut*" (it was added to this, that) ="*moreover,*" or, *in addition to this.* "*Rari*"="in small bodies." "*Alios a. d. excip*"="they relieved *one another* in succession." 91. "*Subsidio confisi*"="confident *of* support." 92. "Summis copiis"="with their *combined* forces." 93. "*Præfixis*"="pointing *outward;*" "*defixæ*"="pointing upward." 94. "*Ripas dimitterent*"="*abandoned* the banks." Not a common meaning of the verb.

95. "*Contentionis*"="a *pitched* battle." 96. "*Agmine*"

="the *main body.*" "*Agmen*"="an army *on its march ;*" "*acies*"="when drawn up *in line.*" 97. "*Tantum— noceretur, quantum,*"="and only so much *mischief was done—*as." 98. "*Vallo atque fossa.*" The *vallum* was a bank formed by the earth dug out of the *fossa,* and planted with stakes "*valli.*" Each soldier carried a certain number of these stakes, with which to fortify the camp ; and this was done whenever the troops halted, though only for a single night. 99. "*Id f. p. extrahi*"="that this might easily be *wasted.*"

LATIN GENDERS.

FIRST DECLENSION.

Feminine.

SECOND DECLENSION.

Masculine Endings, er, ir, *and* us. *Neuter Ending*, um.

Exceptions { alvus, colus (m), domus, humus, vannus; PELAGUS, VIRUS, VULGUS (m)
{ *Greek nouns in* odus, *as* exodus, &c., *with* dialectus, diphthongus, &c.

THIRD DECLENSION.

Masculine endings.	*Feminine Endings.*	*Neuter Endings.*
er, or, os	do, go, io, aa, ia, aus, x	c, a, t, e, l, n
es, *imparisyllabic*	es, *parisyllabic*; s, *impure*	ar, ur, us *short*,
o, *when not* do, go, io	us *long, in hypermonosyllables*	us *long, in mono-*
		syllables

Principal Exceptions.		*Principal Exceptions.*			*Principal exceptions.*	
er CADAVER ITER	do cardo	ordo	udo	*l* sal	sol
PAPAVER TUBER	.go harpago	ligo	margo	*n* lien	pecten
UBER VER	io *nouns not abstract, as* papilio, &c.;			ren	splen
VERBER	also ternio, &c.				
or arbor ÆQUOR	aa aa	elephas	vas (vadis)	*ur* fur	furfur
COR MARMOR	VAS (VASIS)	VAS	NEFAS	turtur	vultur
	is amnis	anguis (f)	axis	cassis (is)		
os oos dos	cinis	collis	crinis	ensis	*us short*, lepus pecus
CHAOS EPOS	fascis	finis (f)	follis	funis	(udia)
OS (ORIS) OS (OSSIS)	ignis	lapis	mensis	orbis	
	panis	piscis	postis	pulvis	*us long*, grus (m)
es compes -meroes	sanguis	torris	unguis	vectis	sus (m) mus
merges quies	vermis				
requies seges	*x* calix	codex	cortex	frutex	
teges æs	grex	pollex	silex	thorax	
	vertex				
o caro echo	*es* acinaces				
	s bidens (f) dens		fons	hydrops	
	mons	pons	rudens (f)		

FOURTH DECLENSION.

Masculine, *except* aous, idus (pl.), manus, porticus, tribus.

FIFTH DECLENSION.

Feminine, *except* dies (f. in sing.), meridies.

~~~~~~~~~~

A. Masculine *by meaning*. Names of Male persons, the occupations of men, and winds, rivers, and months.

B. **Feminine** „ „ of Females, Countries, Islands, Towns, Plants, and Trees.

Masculine......................EXCEPTIONS TO B.....................NEUTER.

Towns. *Some in* o, *as* Croto, Hippo, &c.	TOWNS. *All in* UM, *or plural* A.
All plurals in i, *as* Veii, Delphi, &c.	*Those in* E *or* UR *of the third.*
Plants. *Those in* er (*and many in* us) *of*	PLANTS. *Those in* ER *or* UR *of the third.*
the second.	

VOCABULARY.

ABBREVIATIONS.—With verbs *tr.* means transitive, *int.* intransitive, *dep.* deponent, *n. p.* neuter passive, *def.* defective, *imp.* impersonal, *freq.* frequentative. The numerals 1, 2, 4, show that the verbs are formed *exactly* like *amo, moneo,* and *audio,* or their passives.

The gender of nouns must be learned from the table.

A.

Abdo *see* Do
Abeo *see* Eo
Abies, ĕtis, a fir tree
Abjicio *see* Jacio
Abscindo *see* Scindo
Absisto *see* Sto
Absum *see* Sum
Ac, *conj.* and
Accēdo *see* Cedo
Accĭdo *see* Cado
Accipio *see* Capio
Accūso 1. *tr.* I accuse, blame
Achilles, *is,* a Grecian hero
Acies, ēi, the edge of a weapon, an army in line
Acrĭter, *adv.* sharply
Actus *see* Agere
Acūtus, *adj.* sharp
Adæquo 1. *tr.* I equal, keep up with
Addūco *see* dūco
Adeo, *adv.* so
Adeo *see* Eo
Adhibeo *see* Habeo
Adhuc, *adv.* hitherto
Adĭtus, *us,* an approach, entrance
Adjicio *see* Jacio
Administratio, ōnis, management, execution
Administro *see* Ministro
Admitto *see* Mitto
Admŏdum, *adv.* very much, very
Adolescens, *entis,* a youth

Adorior *see* Orior
Adsum *see* Sum
Adventus, *us,* arrival
Adverto *see* Verto
Advŏlo 1. *int.* I fly to
Ædificium, *i,* a building
Æduus, *i,* an Eduan
Ægre, *adv.* with difficulty
Æquālis, *adj.* equal, of the same age or rank
Æquinoctium, *i,* the Equinox,
Æquus, *adj.* equal, favourable, just
Æs, *ris,* brass, money
Æstas, ātis, summer
ÆSTIMO 1. *tr.* I esteem, value
    Existĭmo, I judge, think
Æstus, *us,* heat, the tide
Ætas, ātis, age, time of life
Æther, ĕris, acc. ēra, the upper region
Affĕro *see* Fero
Afflicto 1. *tr. freq.* of Affligo, I vex, toss
Affligo *see* Fligo
Africa, *æ,* Africa, *Africus, adj.* Africus (ventus *und.*), the south-west wind
Ager, *ri,* a field, territory
Agger, ĕris, a mound
Aggrĕgo *see* Grego
Agmen, ĭnis, a troop, an army on its march; primum *agmen,* the van, novissimum *agmen,* the rear
Agnosco *see* Nosco

Ago, *ĕre*, egi, actum, I put in motion. See App. I. note 28.

Cogo, *(con, ago) ĕre*, coēgi, coactum, *tr.* I drive *together*, collect, compel

Aio, *def.* I say

Alacrĭtas, *ātis*, cheerfulness

Albus, *adj.* white

Aliēnus, *adj.* belonging to another, unfit, unfavourable

Aliquamdiu, *adv.* for a considerable time

Aliquantus, *adj.* some

Alĭquis, *adj.* some, any

Alius, *adj.* another, of many

Alo, *ĕre*, alui, alitum *or* altum, I feed

Alter, *adj.* another *of two*, the second

Altitŭdo, *dĭnis*, height, depth

Altus, *adj.* high, deep

Amens, *adj.* distracted

Amicitĭa, *æ*, friendship

Amitto *see* Mitto

Amor, *ōris*, love

Amplus, *adj.* large, full, noble

An, *conj.* whether, or

Anchŏra *or* Ancŏra, *æ*, an anchor

Angŭlus, *i*, a corner, angle

Angustus, *adj.* narrow

Anĭma, *æ*, breath, the spirit

Animadverto *see* Verto

Anĭmal, *ālis*, an animal

Anĭmus, *i*, the mind, soul, courage

Annŭlus, *i*, a ring

Annus, *i*, a year

Anser, *ĕris*, a goose

Antea, *adv.* before, formerly

Apertus, *part.* open

Appello 1. I call, call by name

Appello 3. *see* Pello

Appōno *see* Pono

Appropinquo 1. *tr.* I approach

Aptus, *adj.* fit, suitable

Aqua, *æ*, water

Aquĭla, *æ*, an eagle

Arbitror 1. *tr. dep.* I think, judge

Arbor *or* Arbos, *ŏris*, a tree

Arceo 2. *tr.* (no *sup.*) I keep off Exerceo. *sup.*—ĭtum, I exercise, employ, train

Arcesso, *ĕre*, ivi, ītum, I send for

Arĭdus, *adj.* dry, parched

Ariovistus, *i*, a German king

Arma, *pl. only*, arms, armour

Armamenta, *pl.* equipment, tackling

Armatūra, *æ*, armour

Armo, 1. *tr.* I arm, equip

Arvum, *i*, a meadow

Aspectus, *us*, sight, appearance

Aspĭcio *see* Spēcio

At, *conj.* but

Ater, *adj.* black

Athēnæ, *pl. only*, Athens

Atque, *conj.* and

Atrĭus, *i*, (Q) a Roman officer

Attingo, *see* Tango

Auctorĭtas, *ātis*, authority

Audacter, *adv.* boldly; *comp.*—acius ; *sup.*—acissime

Audeo, *ēre*, ausus sum, *n. p.* I dare

Auditio, *ōnis*, a report, hearing

Aurĭga, *æ*, one who drives a chariot

Aut, *conj.* either, or

Autem, *conj.* but, for, &c.

Auxilior 1. *int. dep.* I assist

Auxilium, *i*, aid, an auxiliary force

Averto *see* Verto

B.

Barbărus, *adj.* barbarian, rude

Belgæ, *pl.* inhabitants of Northern Gaul

Bellĭcus, *adj.* warlike

Bellua, *æ*, a beast

Bellum, *i*, war

Beneficium, *i*, an act of kindness

Bibracte, *is*, a town in Gaul

Bini, *pl.* two at a time, two

Brevis, *adj.* short

Britannia, *æ*, Britain

Britannus, *i*, a Briton

Bruma, *æ*, the winter solstice, winter

Brundusium, *i*, a town in Italy

F

C.

CADO, *ĕre*, cecĭdi, cāsum, *int.* I fall
Accĭdit, *pres. and perf.* it falls
  out, happens
Occĭdo, *cĭdi, cāsum,* fall, fall
  dead, die, set
CÆDO, *ĕre,* cecĭdi, cæsum, *tr.* I cut,
  k ll
Occīdo, *cīdi, cīsum,* cut down,
  kill
Recīdo—cut *back,* prune, lop off
Cæsar, ŏris, (C. Julius)
Cantium, i, Kent
Capillus, *i,* a hair
CAPIO, *ĕre,* cepi, captum, *tr.* I
  take
Accipio, *cepi, ceptum, tr.* take
  to me, receive
Incipio, take *on* me, begin
Recipio, take *back,* recover,
  draw back; *se recipere,* to
  withdraw
Suscipio, take up, undertake
Captīvus, *i,* a captive
Caput, *ĭtis,* the head
Careo 2. *int.* (*sup.* carītum *or*
  cassum) I am without, am
  free from
Caro, *nis,* flesh
Cassivellaunus, i, a British chief
Castra, *pl. only,* a camp
Casus, *us,* a fall, chance, accident
Causa, *æ,* a cause; *abl.* for the
  sake of
CEDO, *ĕre,* cessi, cessum, *int.* I
  change place, yield
Accēdo, approach, *imp.* it is
  added
Concēdo, give up, grant, depart
Decēdo, go from *or* away, die
Discēdo, go apart, depart
Procēdo, go *before or forward,*
  proceed, advance
Succēdo, come *up,* take the
  place of, succeed
Celerĭtas, *ātis,* speed
Celerĭter, *adv.* speedily
Celo 1. *tr.* I conceal
Cenimagni, pl. a British tribe
Centum, *ind.* a hundred
Certe, *adv.* certainly

CERNO, *ĕre,* (crēvi, crētum, *used
  only in the compounds) tr.*
  separate, distinguish ; see
  Decerno, I determine, decree
Certus, *adj.* certain, accurate,
  undoubted ; *certiorem facere,*
  to inform ; *certior fieri,* to be
  informed
Circĭter, *adv.* about
Circuĭtus, *us,* circuit
Circumsisto *see* Sto
Cito, *adv.* quickly, soon
Civis, *is,* a citizen
Civĭtas, *ātis,* a state, city
Clam, *adv.* secretly
Classis, *is,* a fleet
CLAUDO, *ĕre,* clausi, clausum,
  tr. I shut
Interclūdo, *ĕre, clūsi, clūsum,* I
  shut out, shut up, cut off
Præclūdo, shut out, block up
Coactus, *see* Cogo
Cœlātor, *ōris,* a carver *or* chaser
Cœpi, *or,* cœptus sum, *esse, int.
  def.* I begin
Cœruleus, *adj.* azure, sky-coloured
Cognosco *see* Nosco
Cogo *see* Ago
Cohors, *ortis,* a cohort
Cohortor *see* Hortor
Collēga, *æ,* a colleague
Collĭgo *see* Lego
Collis, *is,* a hill
Collŏco *see* Loco
Collŏquor *see* Loquor
COLO, *ĕre,* cŏlui, cultum, *tr.* I
  cultivate, worship
Incŏlo, I cultivate *in;* dwell in,
  inhabit
Color, *ōris,* colour
Commacŭlo 1. *tr.* I spot, defile
Commeātus, *us,* passage, stores
Commendo, *see* Mando
Commilĭto, *ōnis,* a fellow soldier
Committo *see* Mitto
Commius, i, a Gallic chief
Commŏde, *adv.* conveniently
Commŏdus, *adj.* convenient, ad-
  vantageous
Commūnis, *adj.* common, general
Commutatio, *ōnis,* change
Compăro *see* Paro

Compello *see* Pello
Comperio, *īre, i, tum, tr.* I find out
Compleo *see* Pleo
Compŏno *see* Pono
Complūres, *adj. pl. only,* very many, several
Comprehendo *see* Prehendo
Comprĭmo *see* Premo
Concĕdo *see* Cedo
Concursus, *us,* a rushing together, collision
Confĕro *see* Fero
Confertus, *adj.* crowded, in close array
Confestim, *adv.* immediately
Conficio *see* Facio
Confīdo *see* Fīdo
Confirmo *see* Firmo
Conflīgo *see* Fligo
Congredior *see* Gradior
Congrĕgo *see* Grego
Congressus, *us,* a meeting, interview, encounter
Conjicio *see* Jacio
Conjungo *see* Jungo
Conscendo *see* Scando
Conscisco *see* Scio
Conscrībo *see* Scribo
Consĕquor *see* Sequor
Consīdo *see* Sīdo
Consilium, *i,* advice, design, plan
Consimĭlia, *adj.* like
Consisto *see* Sto
Conspicio *see* Specio
Conspĭcor 1. *tr. dep.* I behold, perceive, *freq.* of Conspicio
Constat *see* Sto
Constituo *see* Statuo
Consuesco *see* Suesco
Consuetūdo, *inis,* a custom
Consul, *ŭlis,* a consul
Consŭlo, *ĕre, ui, tum, tr.* I consult, *int.* I deliberate, consult the interests of
Consulto, *adv.* on purpose
Consultum, *i,* a decree, deliberation
Consūmo *see* Sumo
Contemno, *nĕre, psi, ptum, tr.* I despise
Contendo *see* Tendo
Contentio, *ōnis,* a contest

Contestor 1. *tr.* I call to witness
Contĭnens, *part.* uninterrupted, adjoining ; *continens* (terra *und.*), the continent
Contineo *see* Teneo
Continuus, *adj.* constant, successive
Contumelia, *æ,* insult, injury
Convenio *see* Venio
Convŏco *see* Voco
Coorior *see* Orior
Copia, *æ,* plenty, *pl.* troops, forces
Cor, *dis,* the heart
Coram, *adv.* before one's eyes
Corpŭs, *ŏris,* a body
Creber, *adj.* frequent, crowded
Crimen, *inis,* a charge, crime
Culpa, *æ,* a fault, blame
Cultus, *us,* cultivation, civilization, worship, mode of living, dress
Cuncto 1. *int. dep.* I delay
Cunctus, *adj.* all, the whole
Cupĭde, *adv.* eagerly, keenly
Cupīdo, *inis,* a desire, love
Cupĭdus, *adj.* desirous, eager, fond
Cupio, *ere,* cupīvi, cupītum, *tr.* I desire, covet
Cur, *adv.* why?
Cura, *æ,* care, attention
Curo 1. *tr.* I take care of, cause
CURRO, *ĕre,* cucurri, cursum, *int.* I run
 Occurro, *perf.* occurri or occucurri, run *in the way of,* meet, encounter, oppose
 Percurro, run *through, over* or *along ;* traverse
Currus, *us,* a chariot, car
Cursus, *us,* a race, speed, course, voyage

D.

Debeo 2. *tr.* I owe, ought
Decĕdo *see* Cedo
Decem, *adj.* ten
Decerno *see* Cerno
Decĭmus, *adj.* tenth
Declīvis, *adj.* sloping downwards

Decŭs, ŏris, ornament, dignity
Dedĕcŭs, ŏris, dishonour, disgrace
Deditio, ōnis, surrender
Dedo *see* Do
Dedūco *see* Duco
Defatīgo 1. *tr.* I weary
Defectio, ōnis, a failure, revolt
Defendo *see* Fendo
Defĕro *see* Fero
Deficio *see* Facio
Defīgo *see* Figo
Deinceps, *adv.* in turn
Deinde, *adv.* then, secondly
Dejicio *see* Jacio
Delecto 1. *tr.* I give delight, please
   Delectur, I take delight
Delīgo 1. *see* Ligo
Delīgo 3. *see* Lego
Deliteo *and* Delitesco *see* Lateo
Demeto *see* Meto
Demonstro *see* Monstro
Densus, *adj.* think, crowded
Depereo *see* Eo
Deplŏro *see* Ploro
Depōno *see* Pono
Descendo *see* Scando
Desĕro *see* Sero
Desidĕro 1. I desire, long for,
   pass. to be missing
Desilio *see* Salio
Desisto *see* Sto
Despĕro *see* Spero
Desum *see* Sum
Detestabīlis, *adj.* detestable
Detrimentum, *i*, loss, damage
Deus, *i*, a god
Dico 1. I say, devote
   Judĭco, (jus) administer justice,
     judge
   Prædĭco, say *openly*, declare,
     proclaim,
Dico. ĕre, dixi, dictum, *tr.* I say,
   tell
   Prædĭco, say *beforehand*, foretell
Dies, ēi, a day, season
Differo, *see* Fero
Difficīlis, *adj.* difficult, hard,
   morose
Difficultas, ātis, difficulty
Dignĭtas, ātis, dignity, rank
Diligentia, *æ*, diligence
Dilīgo, *see* Lego

Dimĭco, āre, avi or ui, ātum, *int.*
   I fight
Dimidium, *i*, the half
Dimitto *see* Mitto
Discēdo *see* Cedo
Disciplīna, *æ*, instruction, disci-
   pline, system of training
Disco, ĕre, didĭci, *tr.* I learn
   Perdisco, learn thoroughly *or*
     by heart
Dispar, *adj.* unlike, unequal
Dispergo, *see* Spargo
Dispōno *see* Pono
Distribuo *see* Tribuo
Diu, *adv.* a long time, *comp.* diu-
   tius, *sup.* diutissime
Divĭdo, ĕre, divīsi, divīsum, *tr.* I
   divide
Do, ăre, dĕdi, datum, *tr.* I put,
   give
   Abdo, dĕre, dĭdi, dĭtum, put
         from me, hide
   Condo, „   „ put *together*,
     build, found, conceal
   Dedo, give *up*, surrender
   Perdo, destroy, ruin, lose
   Prodo, give forth *or* up, betray,
     deliver
   Reddo. give *back*, restore,
     render
   Vendo (venum), put to sale, sell
Doceo 2. *sup.* doctum, I teach,
   inform, state
Dolor, ōris, grief, pain
Domestĭcus, *adj.* domestic, in-
   testine
Domus, *us* or *i*, a house, home
Dubĭto 1. *int.* I doubt, hesitate
Dubius, *adj.* doubtful
Ducenti, *adj.* two hundred
Duco, ĕre, duxi, ductum, *tr.* I
   lead
   Addūco, lead *to*, *in*, or *into*, in-
     duce
   Condūco, lead *together*, hire
   Dedūco, lead *down*
   Edūco, lead *out*
   Perdūco, lead *through*, persuade
   Prodūco, lead *forward*, lengthen
   Redūco, lead *back*
   Subdūco, lead *up*, draw up
   Transdūco, lead *across* or *over*

Duo, *adj.* two.

Duplĭco 1. *tr.* I double

Durus, (Q. Laberius) a Roman tribune

Durus, *adj.* hard

Dux, dŭcis, a leader, guide

E.

Edŭco 1. *tr.* I bring up, educate

Edŭco *see* Duco

Efficio *see* Facio

Effugio *see* Fugio

Effundo *see* Fundo

Egeo 2. *no sup. int.* I am in want of

Egestas, *ātis,* want, scarcity

Egredior *see* Gradior

Egregie, *adv.* excellently

Egressus, *us,* a going out, land-ing

Ejicio *see* Jacio

Emitto *see* Mitto

Enim, *conj.* for, &c.

Ensis, *is,* a sword

Enuntio, *see* Nuntio

Eo, *ire,* ivi, *or* ĭi, ĭtum, *int.* I go

  Abeo, go *from* or *away*

  Adeo, *tr.* go *to* or *towards,* ap-proach, apply to

  Depereo *see* Pereo

  Exeo, go *out,* emigrate

  Ineo, *tr.* I go *into,* enter

  Pereo, go *away utterly;* perish

  Redeo, go *back,* return

  Veneo, (venum), go to sale, am sold

  Transeo, go *across* or *over*

Eo, *adv.* thither

Eōdem, *adv.* at *or* to the same place

Epistŏla, *æ,* a letter

Eques, *ĭtis,* a horseman, horse-soldier

Equester, *or* tris, *adj.* of a horse-man, equestrian

Equĭdem, *conj.* indeed

Equitātus, *us,* cavalry

Equus, *i,* a horse

Ergŏ, *conj.* therefore ; *ergō,* for the sake of

Erĭgo *see* Rego

Eruptio, *onis,* a sally

Essĕdum, *i,* a British chariot

Essedarius, *i,* one who fought from a chariot

Et, *conj.* and, also, even

Etiam, *conj.* also, too, even

Etsi, *conj.* although, even, if

Evenio *see* Venio

Excūso 1. *tr.* I excuse

Exeo *see* Eo

Exerceo *see* Arceo

Exercitatio, *ōnis,* exercise, prac-tice

Exercĭtus, *us,* an army

Exiguus, *adj.* scanty, small

Exilium, *i,* exile

Eximius, *adj.* excellent, dis-tinguished

Existĭmo *see* Æstimo

Exĭtus, *us,* issue, end, death

Expeditio, *ōnis,* haste, an expe-dition

Expedĭtus, *part.* unembarrassed, disentangled, easy

Expello *see* Pello

Explorātor, *ōris,* a scout, spy

Explōro 1. *tr.* I search *or* spy out, examine

Expōno *see* Pono

Expugno *see* Pugno

Exspecto *see* Specto

Exsto *see* Sto

Exterior, *adj. comp.* outer, more remote

Extrăho *see* Traho

Extrēmus, *adj. sup.* outermost, most remote

Exuo, *ĕre, i, utum, tr.* I put or strip off

Exūro, *ĕre,* exussi, exustum, *tr.* I burn up

Exuviæ, *pl. only,* that which is put *or* stripped off, spoils

F.

Fabella, *æ,* a little story

Faber, *ri,* an artificer

FACIO, *ĕre*, fēci, factum, *tr.* I make, do

Confĭcio, *ĕre, fēci, fectum,* make *or* put *together,* compile, complete, put an end to, destroy

Defĭcio, make *down* or *from;* unbind, fail, revolt

Effĭcio, make *out of;* bring to pass, cause, finish

Infĭcio, make *or* put *into;* dip, dye, infect, spoil

Interfĭcio, kill, destroy

Perfĭcio, make *thoroughly;* finish, cause, perform

Refĭcio, make *again,* repair, refit

Factum, *i,* thing done, deed, action

Facultas, *ātis,* opportunity

Fagus, *i,* a beech tree

Fas, *ind.* what is according to divine law; *fas est cui, aby.* may, &c.

Faveo, *ĕre,* favi, fautum, *int.* I favour

Felicĭter, *adv.* happily, fortunately

Felix, *adj.* happy, fortunate

FENDO, *ĕre,* fendi, fensum, *tr. not in use, (probably* I strike*)*

Defendo, I strike *from;* ward off, defend

Offendo, I strike *against;* offend, meet with

Fere, *adv.* almost

FERO, ferre, tŭli, lātum, *tr.* I bring, bear, carry

Ad *or* affĕro, bring *to*

Confĕro, bring *together,* compare

Defĕro, carry *down,* report

Diffĕro, carry *apart;* disperse, defer, *int.* differ

Infĕro, bring *in, on,* or *to,* I begin, infer

Ob *or* Offĕro, bring *in the way of;* present, offer, expose

Perfĕro, bear *through, thoroughly,* or *over;* endure, report

Præfĕro, bear *or* put *before;* prefer

Refĕro, bring *back,* relate, report

Ferreus, *adj.* of iron

Ferrum, *i,* iron

Ferus, *adj.* wild, savage

Fidēlis, *adj.* faithful

Fides, *ei,* faith, fidelity, allegiance, loyalty

FIDO, *ĕre,* fisus sum, *n. p.* trust

Confīdo, trust, put confidence in

FIGO, *ĕre,* fixi, fixum, *tr.* fix

Defīgo, fix *down*

Præfīgo, fix *in front*

Figūra, *æ,* form, shape

Filia, *æ,* daughter; *d.* and *abl.* filiabus

Filius, *i,* son

Finis, *is,* end

Finitĭmus, *adj.* neighbouring

FIO, fiĕri, factus sum, *n. p.* to become, happen, *pass.* of *Facio,* to be made *or* done

Firmĭtas, *ātis,* firmness

Firmiter, *adv.* firmly

Firmus, *adj.* firm, strong

FIRMO 1. *tr.* I make firm

Confirmo, I establish, fix, promise as certain

FLECTO, *ĕre,* flexi, flexum, *tr.* I bend, turn

FLIGO, *ĕre,* flixi, flictum, *tr.* I strike violently

Ad *or* Afflīgo, I strike *against;* shatter

Conflīgo, I strike *together;* engage, fight

Fluctus, *us,* a wave

Flumen, *inis,* a river

Foedus, *adj.* foul, disgraceful

Forte, *adv.* by chance

Fortĭter, *adv.* bravely, *comp.* fortius

Fortūna, *æ,* fortune

Fossa, *æ,* a ditch

FRANGO, *ĕre,* frēgi, fractum, *tr.* I break

Perfringo, break *through*

Frigus, *ŏris,* cold

Frumentor 1. *int. dep.* I get corn

Frumentum, *i,* corn

Fruor, *i,* fructus *and* fruitus sum, *int. dep.* I enjoy

Frustra, *adv.* in vain

Frux, *usually pl.* fruges, *um, f.* any fruit, grain

Fuga, *æ,* flight

Fugio, *ĕre,* fūgi, fŭgĭtum, *tr.* and *int.* I fly, fly from

   Effŭgio, escape, elude

Fugo 1. *tr.* I put to flight

Funda, *æ,* a sling

Fundĭtor, *ōris,* a slinger

Fundo, *ĕre,* fudi, fusum, *tr.* I pour, scatter, rout

   Effundo, pour *out of* or *forth,* scatter, rout

   Perfundo, pour *over,* besprinkle, wet

Fundus, *i,* a farm

Fungor, *i,* functus sum, *int. dep.* I perform, fulfil

   Perfungor, perform *thoroughly*

Funis, *is,* a rope, cable

Funus, *ĕris,* a funeral, death, *pl.* funeral rites

Fūr, *is,* a thief

G.

Gallia, *æ,* Gaul

Gallīna, *æ,* a hen

Gens, *tis,* a house, tribe

Genus, *ĕris,* a kind, sort, race, rank

Germania, *æ,* Germany, *Germani* Germans

Gero, *ĕre,* gessi, gestum, *tr.* I carry on, (see App. I. note 28)

Gradior, *i,* gressus sum, *int. dep.* I step

   Congrĕdior, step *together;* meet, encounter

   Egrĕdior, step *out of;* go out, —*navem,* disembark

   Ingrĕdior, go *into,* enter

   Progrĕdior, go *forward,* advance, proceed

Græcia, *æ,* Greece

Gratia, *æ,* favour, influence; *pl.* thanks

Gratus, *adj.* thankful, agreeable

Gravis, *adj.* heavy, important, difficult, troublesome

Gravĭtas, *ātis,* weight, importance

Grego 1. *(from* grex, a flock*) not in use*

   Aggrĕgo, I gather *to,* join

   Congrĕgo, I gather *together,* assemble

Gubernātor, *ōris,* a pilot

Gusto 1. *tr.* I taste

H.

Habeo 2. *tr.* I have, hold, consider, account

   Adhibeo, hibui, hibĭtum, hold *or* apply *to,* use

   Prohibeo, hold *or* keep *off,* hinder

Habĭto 1. *tr.* I inhabit, dwell at

Haud, *adv.* not

Hector, *ōris,* a Trojan hero

Helvetii, *pl.* the Helvetians, Helvetia nearly = the modern Switzerland

Hibernia, *æ,* Ireland

Hic, *dem. adj.* this

Hic, *adv.* at *or* in this, here

Hiĕmo 1. *int.* I winter

Hiems, *ĕmis,* winter, a storm

Hinc, *adv.* from this, thence

Hispania, *æ,* Spain

Hodie, *adv.* to day, now-a-days

Homo, *ĭnis,* a human being, a man

Honestas, *ātis,* honour *as a principle*

Honor, *ōris,* an honour

Hora, *æ,* an hour

Horrĭdus, *adj.* rough, horrible

Hortor 1. *tr. dep.* I exhort, encourage

   Cohortor, *same as* hortor

Hostis, *is,* a *national* enemy

Huc, *adv.* to this, hither

Humānus, *adj.* like a human being, humane, civilized

Humĕrus, *i,* the shoulder

Humus, *i,* the ground

I.

Ibi, *adv.* there, here
Idem, *adj.* the same
Idoneus, *adj.* fit, suitable
Igĭtur, *conj.* therefore
Ignis, *is,* fire
Ignōro 1. *tr.* I do not know, am
    ignorant of
Ignosco *see* Nosco
Ignōtus, *part.* unknown
Ille, *dem. adj.* that
Illic, *adv.* at *or* in that, there
Illo *and* Illuc, *adv.* to that, thither
Immānis, *adj.* huge, uncouth,
    savage
Immedicabĭlis, *adj.* incurable
Immitto *see* Mitto
Immortālis, *adj.* immortal
Impedītus, *part.* embarrassed,
    entangled, intricate
Imperātor, *ōris,* a commander in
    chief
Imperītus, *adj.* unskilled, un-
    acquainted
Imperium, *i,* command, power,
    empire
Impĕro 1. *tr.* I command
Impĕtus, *us,* impetuosity, attack,
    force
Impōno *see* Pono
Importo *see* Porto
Imprīmis, *adv.* in the first place,
    especially
Improvīsus, *adj.* unforeseen ; *de
    improviso,* unexpectedly
Imprūdens, *adj.* not being aware
Imprudentia, *æ,* thoughtlessness,
    indiscretion
Inānis, *adj.* empty
Incendium, *i,* a conflagration
Incendo, *ěre, i, sum, tr.* to set on
    fire, (usually *from within*)
Incertus, *adj.* uncertain
Incipio *see* Capio
Incĭto 1. *tr.* I urge on, spur, excite
Incognĭtus, *adj.* unknown
Incŏlo *see* Colo
Incolŭmis, *adj.* safe
Incommŏdum, *i,* disadvantage,
    loss
Incursio, *ōnis,* inroad

Inde, *adv.* from that, thence
Induo, *ěre, i, tum, tr.* I put on
Ineo *see* Eo
Infēlix, *adj.* unhappy, unfortunate
Infěro *see* Fero
Infěrus, *adj.* low ; *sup.* infimus *or*
    imus
Inficio *see* Facio
Infinītus, *adj.* boundless
Infirmus, *adj.* feeble
Ingenium, *i,* natural capacity
Ingens, *adj.* huge
Ingrĕdior *see* Gradior
Inimīcus, *adj.* unfriendly
Inīquus, *adj.* unjust, unfavourable
Injuria, *æ,* an injury, wrong
Injuste, *adv.* unjustly
Inquam, *def.* I say
Insěquor *see* Sequor
Insěro *see* Sero
Insinuo 1. *tr.* I wind into,
    insinuate
Insisto *see* Sto
Instituo *see* Statuo
Institutum, *i,* a custom, institu-
    tion
Instruo *see* Struo
Insuefactos, *part.* made ac-
    customed, inured
Insŭla, *æ,* an island
Intěger, *adj.* whole, uninjured
Intellĭgo, *see* Lego
Interclūdo *see* Claudo
Interdum, *adv.* sometimes
Interea, *adv.* meanwhile
Intěrest, *imp.* it concerns, is of
    importance
Interficio *see* Facio
Intěrim, *adv.* meantime
Interior, *adj.* inner
Intermitto *see* Mitto
Interpōno *see* Pono
Interpres, *ětis,* an interpreter
Interrŏgo *see* Rogo
Intervallum, *i,* an interval
Intervenio *see* Venio
Introĭtus, *us,* an entrance
Inusitātus, *adj.* unusual
Inutĭlis, *adj.* useless
Invenio *see* Venio
Ipse, *adj.* self, very, mere
Iste, *dem. adj.* that of yours, that

Ita, *adv.* so, thus
Italia, *æ*, Italy, the country south of the river Rubicon
Ităque, *conj.* therefore
Item, *adv.* also
Iter, *inĕris*, a journey, march, road

J.

Jaceo 2. *int.* I lie
JACIO, *ĕre*, jēci, jectum, *tr.* I throw
  Abjicio, *jeci, jectum*, throw *from* or *away*
  Adjicio, throw *to*, add
  Conjicio, throw *together*, hurl, conjecture
  Dejicio, throw *down*
  Ejicio, throw *or* cast out
  Objicio, throw *in the way of*, object, expose, *pass.* lie in the way
  Projicio, throw *forward* or *forth*, throw, throw away
  Rejicio, throw *back*, reject, repulse
  Subjicio, throw *under*, subdue, expose
Jam, *adv.* now, already
Jubeo, *ēre*, jussi, jussum, *tr.* I order
Judex, *ĭcis*, a judge
Judĭco *see* Dico
Jugum, *i*, a yoke, summit
JUNGO, *ĕre*, junxi, junctum, *tr.* I join
  Conjungo, join *together* so as to form one, unite
Jus, *uris*, right, justice

L.

Labienus, *i*, (I.) One of Cæsar's lieutenants
Labŏro 1. *int.* and *tr.* I labour, labour for
Labrum, *i*, the lip
Lac, *tis*, milk

Lacesso, *ĕre*, ĭvi, ĭtum, *tr.* I harass, provoke
Lapis, *ĭdis*, a stone
Late, *adv.* wide
LATEO 2. (no *sup.*) *int.* I lie hid
  Delitesco, *the same meaning*
Latus, *adj.* wide, broad
Latŭs, *ĕris*, the side, flank
Laudo 1. *tr.* I praise
Laus, *dis*, praise
Legātus, *i*, one who acts for another, a lieutenant, ambassador
Legio, *ōnis*, a legion
Legionarius, *adj.* of a legion
LEGO, *ĕre*, lēgi (*in some compounds* lexi), lectum, *tr.* I gather, choose, read
  Collĭgo, *lēgi*, I gather *together*, collect
  Delĭgo, *lēgi*, I gather *from*, choose
  Dilĭgo, *lexi*, I gather *separately*, love
  Elĭgo, *lēgi*, I gather *out of*, elect
  Intellĭgo, *lexi*, I gather *from among*, am aware of, understand
  Neg (nec) lĭgo, *lexi*, I do *not* gather, neglect
Lenis, *adj.* gentle, mild
Lenĭter, *adv.* gently, mildly, *comp.* lenius
Lepŭs, *ŏris*, a hare
Lex, *ēgis*, a law
Libenter, *adv.* willingly
Liber, *adj.* free
Liber, *ri*, a book
Liberalĭter, *adv.* liberally
Libĕre, *adv.* freely
Libĕri, *pl. only*, children
Libĕro 1. *tr.* I set free
Libertas, *ātis*, liberty
Libet, *ēre*, uit, or *ĭtum est*, *imp. int.* it pleases
Licet, *ēre*, uit or *ĭtum est*, *imp. int.* it is permitted
LIGO 1. *tr.* I bind
  Delĭgo, I bind *down*, make fast
LINQUO, *ĕre*, lĭqui, lictum, *tr.* I leave
  Relinquo, leave *behind*, abandon

Liquĭdus, *adj.* liquid

Litĕra, *æ*, a letter of the alphabet, *pl.* an epistle

Lit*ŭs* or Litt*ŭs*, *ŏris*, the shore

Loco 1. *tr.* I place

Coll*ŏco*, I place *together*

Locus, *i*, a place ; *pl.* loci *and* loca

Longe, *adv.* afar, far ; *comp.* longius

Longinquus, *adj.* long, distant

Longitŭdo, *ĭnis*, length

Longus, *adj.* long

Loquor, *i*, locūtus sum ; *tr. dep.* I speak

Coll*ŏquor*, I speak *together*, confer

Lūdo, *ĕre*, *si*, *sum*, *int.* and *tr.* I play, play at

Lumen, *ĭnis*, light

Lūna, *æ*, the moon

M.

Magnifĭcus, *adj.* magnificent, pompous

Magnopĕre, *adv.* with great exertion, too much

Magnus, *adj.* great

Malefĭcium, *i*, mischief

Mandātum, *i*, charge, ínstruction

Mando 1. *tr.* I give charge

Comm*endo*, I entrust, recommend

Mandubratius, *i*, a British chieftain

Mane, *adv.* in the morning

Maneo, *ĕre*, mansi, mansum, *int.* I remain ; *tr.* I await

Perm*aneo*, abide, continue

Rem*aneo*, remain

Manus, *us*, the hand, a band

Maritĭmus, *adj.* maritime

Materia, *æ*, timber

Matūre, *adv.* early, speedily

Matūrus, *adj.* ripe, early, prompt

Maxĭme, *adv.* very much, chiefly, especially

Mediterraneus, *adj.* inland

Medius, *adj.* middle

Membrum, *i*, a limb

Memoria, *æ*, memory, remembrance

Mercātor, *ōris*, a merchant

Meridiānus, *adj.* of noon

Meridies, *ei*, mid-day, the south

Meto, *ĕre*, messui, messum, *tr.* I reap

Demĕto, I reap *off*, *i.e.*, reap *and carry away*

Metus, *us*, fear

Militia, *æ*, military service ; *militia*, in the field

Mille, *adj.* a thousand

Minĭtor 1. *freq.* of Minor

Minister, *ri*, an assistant, attendant

Ministro 1. execute orders, attend upon

Administro, attend to, manage *or* govern according to instructions *or* law

Minor 1. *tr. dep.* I threaten

Miser, *adj.* wretched, miserable

Misereor, *ēri*, *itus* or *tus sum*, *int. dep.* I pity

Mitto, *ĕre*, mīsi, missum, *tr.* I send, throw

Admitto, throw *to* ; apply, admit, permit

Amitto, throw *away* ; lose

Committo, set *together* ; join, entrust, *int.* to act in such a manner

Demitto, send *or* let down ; thrust down

Dimitto, send *apart* ; dismiss, abandon

Emitto, send *out*, or *forth*

Immitto, send *in* or *against* ; insert, put on, relax

Intermitto, send *between*, break off, leave off *or* out, *int.* cease

Permitto, send *through* ; entrust, permit, resign

Præmitto, send *before*, or *forward*

Promitto, send *forth* ; promise, let down

Remitto, send *back* ; abate, slacken

Submitto, put *under*, send up

Mobilĭtas, *ātis*, agility, fickleness
Modĕror 1. *tr. dep.* I guide, check
Modĭus, *i*, a bushel
Molestia, *æ*, vexation, annoyance
Mollis, *adj.* soft, effeminate
Mona, *æ*, an island between Britain and Ireland
Mons, *tis*, a mountain
MONSTRO 1. *tr.* I show
  Demonstro, I point out
Mora, *æ*, delay
Morĭor, *i* or *iri, tuus sum, int. dep.* I die
Moror 1. *int. dep.* I delay; *tr.* I keep waiting
Mors, *tis*, death
Mortālis, *adj.* mortal
Motus, *us*, motion, commotion
MOVEO, *ēre*, mōvi, mōtum, *tr.* I move, *(put in motion)*
  Permŏveo, move *thoroughly;* disturb, surprise, persuade
  Remŏveo, move *back*, withdraw, remove
  Submŏveo, move forcibly, disperse
Mulĭer, *ĕris*, a woman
Multitūdo, *ĭnis*, a great number, a multitude
Multus, *adj.* much, *pl.* many
Mundus, *i*, the world
Munio 4. *tr.* I fortify
Munitĭo, *ōnis*, fortification
Munŭs, *ĕris*, gift, duty, office
Murus, *i*, a wall
Muto 1. *tr.* I change

N.

Nam *and* Namque, *conj.* for
Nanciscor, *i*, nactus sum, *tr. dep.* I meet with, obtain, gain
Nascor, *i*, natus sum, *int. dep.* I am born
Natūra, *æ*, nature
Natus *see* Nascor
Nauta *and* Navita, *æ*, a sailor
Navālis, *adj.* naval
Navigatio, *ōnis*, sailing, a voyage
Navigĭum, *i*, a small ship

Navĭgo 1. *int.* I sail, *tr.* I sail over
Navis, *is*, a ship
Ne, *conj.* that—not, lest
Ne, *enclitic*, whether
Neapŏlis, *is*, Naples
Nec, *conj.* neither, nor
Necessario, *adv.* of necessity
Necesse, *adj.* necessary
Neco, *āre*, avi and ui, *ātum, tr.* I kill
Nefarius, *adj.* sinful
Nefas, *ind.* the opposite to *as*, a sin
Neglĭgo, *see* Lego
Negotium, *i*, business, trouble
Nemo, *ĭnis*, nobody
Nequāquam, *adv.* by no means
Neque, *conj.* the same as *Nec*
Nequitia, *æ*, badness, a bad course of life
Neu, *conj.* neither, nor
Nihil *or* nil, *ind.* nothing
Nimbus, *i*, a storm-cloud, cloud
Nisi, *conj.* unless
Noceo 2. *int.* I hurt
Noctu, *adv.* by night
Nocturnus, of *or* in the night
Nomen, *ĭnis*, a name
Nondum, *adv.* not yet
Nonnullus, *adj.* some
Nonnunquam, *adv.* sometimes
Nonus, *adj.* the ninth
Nosco, *ĕre*, nōvi, nōtum, *tr.* (for gnosco), I obtain information about, become acquainted with; *therefore* novi, I *have* obtained, &c. *or* I know
  Ad *or* Agnosco, *sup.* agnĭtum, I recognise, acknowledge
  Cognosco, *sup.* cognĭtum, I endeavour to obtain information, investigate, *perf.* I know
  Ignosco, *int.* forgive
Novĭtas, *ātis*, novelty
Novus, *adj.* new
Nox, *ctis*, night
Nullus, *adj.* no, none
Num, *conj.* whether
Numĕrus, *i*, a number
Nummus, *i*, money

Nunc, *adv.* now
Nunquam, *adv.* never
NUNTIO 1. *tr.* I bring word, tell, report
   Enuntio, tell *forth*, announce, enounce
   Renuntio, bring word *back*
Nuntius, *i*, a messenger, news
Nutus, *us*, a nod, will

O.

Objicio *see* Jacio
Obliviscor, *i*, *oblitus sum*, *int.* and *tr.* I forget
Obses, *ĭdis*, a hostage
Obtempĕro *see* Tempĕro
Occāsus, *us*, a fall, setting
Occĭdo *see* Cado
Occīdo *see* Cædo
Occulto 1. *tr.* I hide
Occupatio, *ōnis*, seizure, employment
Occŭpo 1. *tr.* I seize, occupy
Occurro *see* Curro
Oceǎnus, *i*, the ocean
Ocŭlus, *i*, the eye
Offendo *see* Fendo
Offĕro *see* Fero
Officium, *i*, a duty, office, kindness
Omnīno, *adv.* altogether, in all, at all
Omnis, *adj.* all every
Onerarius, *adj.* of burden
Onŭs, *ĕris*, a burden, load
Opĕra, *æ*, labour, exertion ; *dare operam*, to exert oneself
Opinio, *ōnis*, reputation, opinion
Opīnor 1. *tr.* I think
Oportet, *ēre*, *uit.* *imp.* *tr.* it behoves
Oppidānus, *adj.* of a town
Oppĭdum, *i*, a town
Opportūnus, *adj.* fit, seasonable
Opprimo *see* Premo
Oppugnatio, *ōnis*, assault, siege
Oppugno *see* Pugno
Optĭme, *adv.* best, very well

Opŭs, *ĕris*, a work
Opus, *ind.* need ; *ind.* *adj.* necessary
Ora, *æ*, coast
Oratio, *ōnis*, a speech
Orbis, *is*, a circle, the world
Ordo, *ĭnis*, order, rank
ORIOR, orīri, ortus sum, 3 and 4. *int.* I rise, spring, am born
   Adorior, *tr.* fall upon, attack
   Coorior, *int.* arise
Ornamentum, *i*, ornament, dignity
Oro 1. I pray, entreat
Ortus, *us*, rising, birth
Os, *ris*, the mouth, countenance
Ostendo *see* Tendo
Otium, *i*, ease, idleness
Otiōsus, *adj.* at leisure, idle

P.

Pabulātor, *ōris*, a forager
Pabulor 1. *int.* *dep.* I get in forage
Palūs, *ūdis*, a marsh, fen
Par, *adj.* equal, like
Parco, *ĕre*, peperci, parcĭtum *and* parsum, *int.* I spare
Parens, *tis*, a parent
PARO 1. *tr.* I make ready
   Compăro, compare, procure
   Præpăro, make ready *beforehand*, prepare
Pars, *tis*, a part
Parvus, *adj.* small, little
Passus, *us*, a step—about 5ft. English
PATIOR, *i*, passus sum, *tr.* *dep.* I suffer
   Perpetior, *i*, pessus sum, suffer greatly, endure
Patria, *æ*, native country
Pauci, *pl.* *adj.* few
Paucĭtas, *ātis*, smallness, small number, scarcity
Paullātim, *adv.* little by little
Paulisper, *adv.* a little while
Paulo *and* Paulum, *adv.* a little
Paulŭlum, *adv.* very little
Pax, *ācis*, peace

Pecūs, ŏris, sheep, flock

Pedes, ĭtis, a foot soldier

Pedester *and* tris, *adj.* on foot, pedestrian

Peditātus, *us*, infantry

Pellis, *is*, skin, hide

PELLO, *ĕre*, pepuli, pulsum, *tr.* I drive

  Appello, *pŭli, pulsum*, drive *to* or *towards*

  Compello, drive *together*, compel

  Expello, drive *out of*

  Impello, drive *into, on* or *against*

  Repello, drive *back*, repulse, reject

Pendo, *ĕre*, pependi, pensum, *tr.* I weigh, pay

Percontatio, *ōnis*, enquiry

Percurro *see* Curro

Perdisco *see* Disco

Perdūco *see* Duco

Pereo *see* Eo

Perequĭto 1. *int.* I ride through *or* about

Perfĕro *see* Fero

Perficio *see* Facio

Perfringo *see* Frango

Perfŭga, *æ*, a deserter, fugitive

Perfundo *see* Fundo

Perfungor *see* Fungor

Periclŭlum, *i*, trial, danger

Permagnus, *adj.* very great

Permaneo *see* Maneo

Perpauci, *pl. adj.* very few

Perpetior *see* Patior

Perpetuus, *adj.* continual ; *in perpetuum*, for ever

Perrumpo *see* Rumpo

Persĕquor *see* Sequor

Perspicio *see* Specio

Persuadeo *see* Suadeo

Perterreo *see* Terreo

Perturbatio, *ōnis*, consternation

Perturbo *see* Turbo

Pervenio *see* Venio

Pes, *ĕdis*, a foot

Peto, *ĕre*, ivi, itum, *tr.* I seek, make for

Philosŏphus, *i*, a philospher

Pinus, *us* and *i*, a fir tree

Planus, *adj.* level, plain

Plenus, *adj.* full

PLEO 2. *not in use*

  Compleo, *ēre, ēvi, ētum*, I fill up, complete

  Impleo, I fill

Plerīque, *pl. adj.* sometimes *sing.* very many, the most part

Plerumque, *adv.* for the most part, generally

PLORO 1. *int.* and *tr.* I weep, lament

  Deplōro, I bewail, lament for

Plumbum, *i*, lead ; *plumbum album*, tin

Plus, *adv.* more, longer

Polliceor, *ēri*, pollicitus sum, *tr. dep.* I promise

Pondero 1. *tr.* I weigh, examine

Pondŭs, *ĕris*, weight

PONO, *ĕre*, posui, posĭtum, *tr.* I put, place

  Ad *or* Appōno, put *to*, apply

  Compōno, put *together*, compose, compare

  Depōno, put *down*, lay aside, deposit

  Dispōno, put *apart*, separate, arrange

  Expōno, put *forth*, explain

  Interpōno, put *between*, interpose

Popŭlus, *i*, a people

Porta, *æ*, a gate

PORTO 1. I carry

  Importo, carry *in* or *into*, import

  Reporto, carry *back*

  Transporto, carry *across* or *over*

Portus, *us*, a harbour

Possum, posse, potui, —, I am able, am powerful

Postea, *adv.* afterwards

Postĕrus, *adj.* following, ensuing ; *sup. postremus* and *postumus*, latest *or* last

Postquam, *adv.* after

Postrēmo, *adv.* lastly

Postridie, *adv.* next day

Postŭlo 1. *tr.* I ask, demand

Potens, *part.* able, powerful

Potestas, *ātis*, power, authority

G

Potior, iri, ïtus sum, int. dep. I
   get possession of, obtain,
   enjoy
Potius, adv. rather
Præceps, cipĭtis, adj. headlong,
   steep
Præclārus, adj. illustrious, dis-
   tinguished
Præclūdo see Claudo
Præda, æ, booty, plunder
Prædīco see Dīco
Prædĭco see Dīco
Prædor 1. int. dep. I get booty
Præfectus, i, a prefect, an officer
   of the allies
Præfĕro see Fero
Præfïgo see Figo
Præmitto see Mitto
Præpăro see Paro
Præsidium, i, protection, garrison
Præsto see Sto
Præsum see Sum
Prætor, ōris, Roman magistrate
   next in rank to the consuls
PREHENDO or PRENDO, ĕre,
   prendi, prensum, tr. lay hold
   of
Comprehendo, seize, apprehend
PREMO, ĕre, pressi, pressum, tr.
   I keep down, press
Comprĭmo, press together, con-
   trol, compel
Opprĭmo, press against, oppress
Pretium, i, price, reward
Pridie, adv. the day before
Primo and primum, adv. at first,
   in the first place
Primus, adj. see Prior
Princeps, cïpis, adj. chief, first
Prior, adj. former; sup. primus
   first
Pristïnus, adj. former, ancient
Prius, adv. formerly
Priusquam, adv. before
Procēdo see Cedo
Procul, adv. far, afar
Prodo see Do
Prœlior 1. int. I fight
Prœlium, i, a battle
Proficiscor, i, profectus sum, int.
   dep. I set out, depart
Progredior see Gradior

Prohibeo see Habeo
Projicio see Jacio
Promitto see Mitto
Propinquus, adj. near, akin
Propior, adj. nearer; sup. prox-
   ïmus, next
Propius, adv. nearer
Proprius, adj. one's own, peculiar,
   proper
Propugno see Pugno
Prosĕquor see Sequor
Prospectus, ūs, a view, prospect
Prosum see Sum
Protïnus, adv. forthwith
Provĕho see Veho
Provideo see Video
Provincia, æ, a province
Proxïmus see Propior
Pudet, ēre, uit, imp. it shames
Pugna, æ, a fight
PUGNO 1. int. I fight
   Expugno, tr. take by assault
   Oppugno, tr. assault, lay siege
   to
   Propugno, int. fight in front,
   resist; tr. to fight for
Pulcher, adj. beautiful, honour-
   able
Pulvis, ĕris, dust
Puto 1. I suppose, think

Q.

Quæro, ĕre, quæsīvi, quæsītum,
   tr. I seek, ask, enquire
Quæstor, ōris, a Roman magis-
   trate, paymaster in the army
Qualis, adj. of what kind
Quam, adv. and conj. how, than, as
Quantus, adj. how much, how
   great
Quare, adv. why, wherefore
Quartus, adj. the fourth
Quasi, conj. as if, as it were
Queror, i, questus sum, int. dep.
   I complain
Qui, adv. how
Quia, conj. because
Quicunque, adj. whosoever
Quid, adv. why

Quiētus, *adj.* quiet, calm
Quin, *conj.* but, but that, why not
Quingenti, *adj.* five hundred
Quinquaginta, *ind. adj.* fifty
Quintus, *adj.* fifth
Quis, *inter. adj.* who? which?
Quis (after *ne, si,* &c.) *indef. adj.* any
Quisquam, *indef. pron.* any one
Quisque, *indef. adj.* each
Quisquis, *indef. adj.* whoever
Quoad, *adv.* until, as far as, whilst
Quomīnus, *conj.* but that
Quomŏdo, *adv.* how
Quondam, *adv.* formerly
Quoniam, *conj.* since
Quot, *adj. ind.* how many
Quotidiānus, *adj.* daily
Quotidie, *adv.* every day, daily
Quoties, *adv.* how many times
Quum, *conj.* when, since, although

R.

Rādo, *ĕre,* rāsi, rāsum, *tr.* I scrape, shave
Rarus, *adj.* thin, rare; *pl.* scattered, few
Ratio, *ōnis,* reason, plan, reckoning, method
Rebellio, *ōnis,* rebellion, revolt
Recens, *adj.* fresh, recent
Receptus, *us,* a place of retreat, refuge
Recīdo *see* Cædo
Recordor 1. *int.* and *tr.* I remember
Rectus, *adj.* right, straight
Recūso 1. *tr.* I refuse
Reddo *see* Do
Redeo *see* Eo
Redītus, *us,* a return, revenue
Redūco *see* Duco
Rĕfĕro *see* Fero
Rĕfert, *imp.* it concerns, is of importance
Regio, *ōnis,* a district, region
Regno 1. *int.* and *tr.* I reign, reign over

Rego 3. I give a direction to, rule
Erĭgo, direct *upwards,* set up, erect
Rejicio *see* Jacio
Relinquo *see* Linquo
Relīquus, *adj.* remaining, left
Remaneo *see* Maneo
Remīgo 1. *tr.* I row
Remigro 1. *int.* I move back
Reminiscor, *i, int. dep.* I recollect
Remitto *see* Mitto
Removeo *see* Moveo
Remus, *i,* an oar
Renuntio *see* Nuntio
Repello *see* Pello
Repente, *adv.* suddenly
Reperio, *īre, i, tum, tr.* I find, find out
Reporto *see* Porto
Res, *ēi,* a thing, an affair, property
Respondeo, *dēre, di, sum, tr.* I answer
Respublīca, *æ,* reipublīcæ, a commonwealth
Retineo *see* Teneo
Reverto *see* Verto
Revŏco *see* Voco
Rex, *rēgis,* a king
Rhodus, i, f. Rhodes
Ripa, *æ,* a bank
Rogo 1. *tr.* I ask
Interrŏgo, ask a question of
Rota, *æ,* a wheel
Rufus, i, (P. Sulpicius) one of Cæsar's lieutenants
Rumor, *ōris,* a report, rumour
Rumpo, *ĕre, rūpi, ruptam, tr.* I break
Perrumpo, break *through*
Rursus, *adv.* again
Rūs, *ūris,* the country

S.

Sabīnus, i, (Q. Titurius) one of Cæsar's lieutenants
Sæpe, *adv.* often
Sagitta, *æ,* an arrow

Sagittarius, *i*, an Archer

SALIO, *īre*, salui *and* salii, saltum, *int.* I leap

Desilio, *sup.* desultum, leap *down*

Sanies, *ēi*, blood, gore

Sanguis, *is*, blood

Sano 1. *tr.* I heal

Satis *and* Sat, *adv.* enough

Scapha, *æ*, a skiff

SCANDO, *ĕre*, scandi, scansum, *tr.* I go by steps

Conscendo, *di*, *sum*, ascend ; *conscendere navem*, embark

Descendo — climb down, descend ; *descendere navem*, disembark

SCINDO, *ĕre*, scĭdi, scissum, *tr.* I cut

Abscindo, cut away, cut off, tear up

SCIO 4. *tr.* I know *a thing*, *freq.* Scisco

Conscisco, unanimously approve of, resolve on ; *consiscere mortem sibi*, to put oneself to death

SCRIBO, *ĕre*, scripsi, scriptum, *tr.* I write

Conscrībo, write *together*, write a list (of names), levy troops

Secundus, *adj.* second, prosperous

Secus, *adv.* otherwise ; *haud secus ac*, just as

Sed, *conj.* but

Seditiōsus, *adj.* seditious

Semel, *adv.* once

Semĭta, *æ*, a path

Semper, *adv.* always

Senātus, *us*, the senate at Rome, a supreme council

Senex, *is*, old

Sensus, *us*, feeling, a sense

Sententia, *æ*, an opinion, sentiment

SENTIO, *īre*, sensi, sensum, *tr.* I perceive by the senses ; am of opinion

Consentio, am of the same opinion, consent

Septem, *adj.* seven

Septemtriōnes, *pl.* the seven stars in the Great Bear, the north

Septĭmus, *adj.* seventh

SEQUOR, *i*, secūtus sum, *tr. dep.* I follow ; *sequitur*, it follows, *int.*

Consĕquor, follow *after*, overtake

Insĕquor, follow *upon*, follow

Persĕquor, follow *up*, pursue

Prosĕquor, accompany, honour with a gift, pursue

Subsĕquor, follow closely

Sermo, *ōnis*, speech, discourse

SERO, *ĕre*, serui, sertum, *tr.* I twine *or* weave

Desĕro, disentwine, loosen, desert

SERO, *ĕre*, sevi, satum, *tr.* I plant, sow

Insĕro, *sēvi*, *sĭtum*, *tr.* I implant

Servio 4. *int.* I am the slave of, serve

Servĭtus, *ūtis*, slavery

Servo 1. *tr.* I keep, save

Sestertius, *i*, a Roman coin

Si, *conj.* if

Sicilia, *æ*, Sicily

SIDO, *ĕre*, sidi *and* sēdi, *no. sup.* *int.* I settle, sink

Consido, *sēdi*, settle *down*, sit down, encamp

Signum, *i*, sign, signal, standard

Silva, *æ*, a wood

Silvester *and* tris, *adj.* woody

Simĭlis, *adj.* like

Similitūdo, *ĭnis*, likeness

Simul, *adv.* at the same time

Singulāris, *adj.* singular, one by one

Sinistra, *æ*, the left hand

Sino, *ĕre*, sivi, situm, *tr.* I suffer, permit

Socius, *i*, a companion, ally

Sol, *olis*, the sun

Solitūdo, *ĭnis*, a solitude, desert

Solon, *ōnis*, an Athenian philosopher and statesman

Solum, *adv.* only

Solvo, *ĕre*, solvi, solūtum, *tr.* I *loosen, pay*

Soror, *ōris*, sister

SPARGO, *ĕre*, sparsi, sparsum, *tr.*
I scatter
Dispergo, *spersi, spersum*, scatter *apart*, disperse
Species, *ēi*, appearance, form, pretence
SPECIO, *ĕre*, spexi, spectum, I look
Aspicio, look *at*, behold
Conspicio, look at (*emphatically*)
Perspicio, look *thoroughly*, see through
Suspicio, look up, suspect
SPECTO 1. *int.* (*freq.* of *specio*), I look at *or* towards
Exspecto, *tr.* I look *out for*, expect, await
Speculatorius, *adj.* used for spying or watching
SPERO 1. *tr.* I hope, hope for
Despēro, leave off hoping, despair
Spes, *ei*, hope
Spolio 1. *tr.* I plunder, strip
Stabilĭtas, *ātis*, firmness
Statim, *adv.* immediately
Statio, *ōnis*, guard, outpost
STATUO, *ĕre*, statui, statūtum, *tr.*
I cause to stand, place, determine
Constituo, place *together*, arrange, draw up, determine
Instituo, place into, determine, begin, establish, construct, train up *or* instruct
STO, *āre*, stĕti, stātum, *int.* I stand
SISTO, *ĕre*, is the *freq.* both of *statuo* and *sto*, and is therefore both *tr.* and *int.* I place, stand
Absisto, *int.* stand *off*
Circumsisto, *tr.* stand *around*
Consisto, *int.* stand *together*, stop, halt
Constat, *imp.* it is evident
Desisto, *int.* leave off, cease
Exsto, *int.* stand out
Insisto, *int.* stand still ; *tr.* press upon, urge, undertake
Præsto, *int.* stand before, be better ; *tr.* perform, display
Subsisto, *int.* stand fast, hold out, exist

Strepĭtus, *us*, din, uproar
STRUO, *ĕre*, struxi, structum, *tr.*
I join together
Instruo, put in order, draw up, build, equip
Studiōsus, *adj.* desirous, careful
Studium, zeal, a pursuit
Stultus, *adj.* foolish
SUADEO, *ēre*, suasi, suasum, *tr.*
I advise
Persuadeo, advise
Subdūco *see* Duco
Subĭto, *adv.* suddenly
Subĭtus, *adj.* sudden
Subjicio *see* Jacio
Sublātus *see* Tollo
Subministro *see* Ministro
Submitto *see* Mitto
Submoveo *see* Moveo
Subsĕquor *see* Sequor
Subsidium, *i*, assistance, reinforcement, a reserve
Subsisto *see* Sto
Succēdo *see* Cedo
Succĭdo *see* Cædo
Sudes, *is*, a stake
SUESCO, *ĕre*, suevi, suetum, *int.*
I become accustomed to, *tr.*
I accustom to
Consuesco, *same as* Suesco
SUM, *verb subst.* I am
Absum, am absent
Adsum, am present
Desum, am wanting
Præsum, am before *or* over, command
Prosum, am serviceable to, do good
Supersum, am over, remain, survive
Summa, *æ*, the sum, the whole
Summus, *adj.* highest, greatest
SUMO, *ĕre*, sumpsi, sumptum, *tr.*
I take
Consūmo, spend, waste, consume
Sumptuōsus, *adj.* expensive
Superior, *adj.* higher, former
Supĕro 1. *tr.* I excel
Supersĕdeo, *ēre*, sēdi, sessum, *tut.*
I refrain from
Supersum *see* Sum

Suppetĕre, ivi, itum, *int.* to be supplied, to be sufficient

Supplicatio, ōnis, a public thanksgiving

Supplicium, i, entreaty, punishment

Supra, *adv.* above, before

Suscipio *see* Capio

Suspicor 1. *freq.* of Suspicio, I suspect, see *Specio*

Sustineo *see* Teneo

Syracūsæ, pl. only, Syracuse

T.

Tabŭla, *æ,* a board, picture, register

Tædet, ēre, tæduit *and* pertæsum est, *imp.* it wearies

Talea, *æ,* a pin or spike

Talis, *adj.* of such kind

Tam, *adv.* so

Tamen, *conj.* however

Tamĕsis, is, the Thames

Tango, ĕre, tetigi, tactum, *tr.* I touch

Attingo, *tigi,* touch, border on

Tanquam, *conj.* as if

Tantus, *adj.* so great, so much

Tarde, *adv.* slowly ; *comp. tardius*

Tarentum, i, a city of Italy

Tectum, i, a roof, house

Tego, ĕre, zi, etum, *tr.* I cover

Telum, i, a weapon, dart

Temĕre, *adv.* rashly, without consideration

Temo, ōnis, a pole of a chariot

Temperantia, *æ,* moderation

Tempero 1. *tr.* and *int.* I moderate, govern, restrain

Obtempĕro, *int.* obey

Tempestas, ātis, time, weather, a storm

Tempŭs, ŏris, time

Tendo, ĕre, tetendi, tentum *and* tensum ; *tr.* I stretch

Contendo, *tendi,* stretch together ; vie, contend, hasten

Ostendo, stretch *in the way of,* hold out, show

Teneo, ēre, tenui, tentum, *tr.* I hold, contain

Contineo, hold *together,* bound, restrain, contain

Retineo, hold *back,* detain, retain

Sus (sub) *tineo,* hold up against, bear up, endure

Tergum, i, the back

Terreo 2. *tr.* I frighten

Perterreo, frighten greatly

Terror, ōris, fright

Tertius, *adj.* third

Testamentum, i, a will

Testūdo, ĭnis, a tortoise, military term

Timor, ōris, fear

Tollo, ĕre, sustŭli, sublātum, *tr.* I lift up, take away, set aside

Tormentum, i, a military engine, torture

Tot, *adj. ind.* so many

Traho, ĕre, traxi, tractum, *tr.* I draw

Extrăho, draw *out,* exhaust

Transdūco *see* Duco

Transeo *see* Eo

Transjectus, us, a carrying over, passage

Transmissus, us, a passage, voyage

Transporto *see* Porto

Trebonius, (C,) one of Cæsar's lieutenants

Tres, *n.* tria, three

Tribūnus, i, a tribune

Tribuo, ĕre, tribui, tribūtum, I give, confer, ascribe

Distribuo, give *amongst,* distribute

Trinobantes, pl. a British tribe

Tripartīto, *adv.* in three divisions

Triquetrus, *adj.* triangular

Triticum, i, wheat

Turbo 1. *tr.* I throw into confusion

Perturbo, throw into great confusion

Turma, *æ,* a troop of horse

U.

Ubi, *adv.* where, when
Ubinam, *adv.* where?
Ullus, *adj.* any
Ulterior, *adj.* farther ; *sup.* ul-
  timus
Ultra, *adv.* beyond
Ultro, *adv.* willingly, spontane-
  ously
Una, *adv.* together
Unda, *æ,* a wave
Unde, *adv.* from which, whence
Undique, *adv.* on every side
Universus, *adj.* all, the whole
Unquam, *adv.* ever
Unus, *adj.* one, alone
Urbs, *is,* a city
Usus, *us,* use, experience, need
Uti, same as *ut*
Uter, *adj.* whether of the two
Uterque, *adj.* both
Utilitas, *ātis,* utility, advantage
Utor, *i,* usus sum, *int. dep.* I use,
  enjoy, practice
Utrinque, *adv.* on both sides
Utrum, *conj.* whether
Uxor, *ōris,* a wife

V.

Vadum, *i,* a shallow, ford
Vagor 1. *int. dep.* I wander
Valeo 2. *int.* I am in health, am
  powerful ; *vale,* farewell
Vallum, *i,* a rampart
Vas, *āsis,* a vessel, vase
Vasto 1. *tr.* I lay waste
Vectigal, *ālis,* tax, tribute
Vectorius, *adj.* fitted to carry ;
  naves vectoriæ, transports
VEHO, *ĕre,* vexi, vectum, *tr.* I
  carry
  Provĕho, carry *forward* or *forth*
Vendo *see* Do
Veneo *see* Eo
Venēnum, *i,* poison

VENIO, *īre,* vēni, ventum, *int.* I
  come
  Convenio, come *together ;* tr.
  call upon ; *imp.* it suits
  Evenio, to come *forth,* happen
  Intervenio, come *between,* be
  present, intervene
  Invenio, come *upon,* find
  Pervenio, come through, make
  one's way
Venor 1. *tr.* and *int. dep.* I hunt
Ventito 1. *freq.* of *Venio,* I come
  often, come to and fro
Ventus, *i,* the wind
Verbum, *i,* a word
Vereor, *ēri,* itus sum, *tr. dep.* I
  fear
Vergĕre, *int.* to incline, lie to-
  wards
Vero *and* verum, *conj.* but, how-
  ever
Vero, *adv.* truly, indeed
VERTO, *ĕre,* verti, versum, *tr.* I
  turn
  Adverto, turn *to*
  Animadverto, turn *one's mind
  to,* observe
  Averto, turn *from,* ward off
  Reverto or vertor, turn *back*
Vertor, *int.* I turn, *pass.* I am
  turned
Verus, *adj.* true, real
VESCOR, *i, int. dep.* I feed on
Vestio 4. *tr.* I clothe
Veto, *āre, ui, itum, tr.* I forbid
Vetus, *ĕris, adj.* old
Vicies, *adj.* twenty times
Vicus, *i,* village, hamlet
VIDEO, *ēre,* vīdi, vīsum, *tr.* I
  see
  Provideo, see *before,* foresee,
  provide
Vigilia, *æ,* watching, a watch
Viginti, *adj.* twenty
Vinco, *ĕre,* vīci, victum, *tr.* I
  conquer
Vinculum, *i,* a bond, chain
Vir, *i,* a man, husband
Virtus, *ūtis,* virtue, courage
Vis, vis, acc. *vim,* ab. *vi,* force,
  violence ; *pl. vires,* strength
Viscus, *ĕris,* usually *pl.* the bowels

Viso, *ĕre, i, um, tr.* I go to see, visit

Vita, *æ,* life

Vito 1. *tr.* I avoid, shun

Vitrum, *i,* woad

Vitta, *æ,* a headband

Vivo, *ĕre,* vixi, victum, *int.* I live

Vivus, *adj.* living

Vix, *adv.* scarcely

Voco 1. *tr.* I call

 Convŏco, call *together,* summon

 Revŏco, call *back,* call again

Volo, velle, volui, *tr.* I wish, am willing

Voluntas, *ātis,* will, desire

Voluptas, *ātis,* pleasure

Volusēnus, i, (C) one of Cæsar's officers

Vulnŭs, *ĕris,* a wound

NUMERAL ADJECTIVES.

	Cardinal.	Ordinal.	Distributive.
1	Unus, *one, &c.*	Primus, *first, &c.*	Singŭli, *one by one, &c.*
2	Duo	Secundus	Bini
3	Tres	Tertius	Terni
4	Quatuor	Quartus	Quaterni
5	Quinque	Quintus	Quini
6	Sex	Sextus	Seni
7	Septem	Septĭmus	Septēni
8	Octo	Octāvus	Octōni
9	Novem	Nonus	Novēni
10	Decem	Decĭmus	Deni
11	Undĕcim	Undecĭmus	Undēni
12	Duodĕcim	Duodecĭmus	Duodēni
13	Tredĕcim	Decĭmus tertius	Tredēni, terni deni
14	Quatuordĕcim	Decĭmus quartus	Quaterni deni
15	Quindĕcim	Decĭmus quintus	Quindēni
16	Sexdĕcim	Decĭmus sextus	Seni deni
17	Septemdĕcim	Decĭmus septĭmus	Septēni deni
18	Octodĕcim, *or* Duodeviginti	Decĭmus octāvus	Octōni deni
19	Novendĕcim *or* Undeviginti	Decĭmus nonus	Novēni deni
20	Viginti	Vigesĭmus, vicesĭmus	Vicēni
21	Viginti unus *or* Unus et viginti	Vigesĭmus primus	Vicēni singŭli
30	Triginta	Trigesĭmus, tricesĭmus	Tricēni
40	Quadraginta	Quadragesĭmus	Quadragēni
50	Quinquaginta	Quinquagesĭmus	Quinquagēni
60	Sexaginta	Sexagesĭmus	Sexagēni
70	Septuaginta	Septuagesĭmus	Septuagēni
80	Octoginta	Octogesĭmus	Octogēni
90	Nonaginta	Nonagesĭmus	Nonagēni
100	Centum	Centesĭmus	Centēni
200	Ducenti	Ducentesĭmus	Ducēni
300	Trecenti	Trecentesĭmus	Trecentēni
400	Quadringenti	Quadrincentesĭmus	Quater centēni
500	Quingenti	Quingentesĭmus	Quinquies centēni
600	Sexcenti	Sexcentesĭmus	Sexies centēni
700	Septingenti	Septingentesĭmus	Septies centēni
800	Octingenti	Octingentesĭmus	Octies centēni
900	Nongenti	Nongentesĭmus	Novies centēni
1000	Mille	Millesĭmus	Millēni
2000	Duo millia, *or* bis mille	Bis millesĭmus	Bis millēni

RULES FOR SCANNING.

---

§ 1. A *Foot* is a combination of two or more syllables contained either in one or in several words.

§ 2. The feet most frequently employed in Latin verse are Dactyls and Spondees.

§ 3. A *Dactyl* consists of *one long* syllable followed by *two short* ones; as " *vincĕrĕ.*" A *Spondee* consists of *two long* syllables; as *vinclūst.*

§ 4. A *Verse* is a combination of two or more feet.

§ 5. The verses which occur most frequently are Hexameters and Pentameters.

§ 6. A *Hexameter* contains *six* feet, of which the last is a spondee, and the last but one is, almost always, a dactyl; the first four are *either* dactyls *or* spondees.

§ 7. A *Pentameter* consists of two halves, each of which *contains two complete* feet and a syllable over. In the *first* half, the feet are either dactyls *or* spondees, and are followed by a long syllable which *always ends a word*. The *second* half must contain two dactyls and a syllable over.

§ 8. In Hexameters and Pentameters the last syllable of the verse is accounted *long*, no matter what its actual quantity may be.

We may now repeat the general rules given in *Page* 1, and add the most important exceptions.

§ 9. A vowel before two consonants, or before *z*, *x*, or *j*, is *long*.

> *Except* (i.) A vowel which is short in the root may, in some cases, remain short in other forms of the word, before a *mute* followed by a *liquid*. Thus we may have *pătris* or *pātris*, because the *a* in *păter* is short; but *mātris* only, because the *a* in *māter* is long.
>
> (ii.) In *bĭjugus*, and other compounds of *jugum*, the vowel before *j* is short.

§ 10. A diphthong is *long*.

> *Except*—In words compounded with *præ* before a vowel the diphthong is short.
>
> *Obs. Qu* is equivalent to a single consonant; thus, *quĕ*, *equŭs.* So also *gu.*

§ 11. A vowel before a vowel is *short*.*

> *Except* (i.) The gen. of *unus*, &c. is " *īus* " or " *ĭus.* " But always *alīus* and *alterĭus.*

---

* *H* is in no case considered a letter.

(ii.) In *fio* and its inflexions, *i* is *long*, when not followed by
er; thus, *fīo*, *fīam*, but *fīerem*.

(iii.) In the gen. and dat. of the fifth, *e* is long when it follows
i; thus, *faciēi*; but, *spei*.

(iv.) *Dĭana* (or *Dīana*), *ōhe* (or *ŏhe*), *ēheu*, *āer*.

§ 12. Quantity of Final Syllables.

The words in italics have the final syllable *common*. A long or
short vowel following such words indicates that, though common, they
are *generally* of that quantity.

LONG ENDINGS.	SHORT ENDINGS.
a, i, o,* u—c, n as, es, os	e—b, d, t, l, r is, us

PRINCIPAL EXCEPTIONS.	PRINCIPAL EXCEPTIONS.
a pută, ită, quiă, posteă, ejă All cases in *a* except the abl. of the first *Contra, juxta*, and *numerals in* "*ginta*" *(ā)* *i* nisĭ, quasĭ *mihi, tibi, sibi, ibi, ubi* *o* *modo, quomodo, &c.* *ambo, duo, ego, homo, illico,* *(ŏ)* and a few others *c* nĕc, donĕc, făc *hic* and *hoc*, when not in the abl. *n* Nomĕn and others which make the gen. in "ĭnis," ăn, forsăn, &c. tamĕn, at- tamĕn, &c. ĭn *as* anăs *es* Nouns in "es" which in- crease short. But cerēs, abiēs, ariēs, pariēs, and pēs with its compounds penēs and ĕs *(thou art)* *os* compŏs, impŏs, ŏs (G. ossis)	*e* Abl. of the fifth, and deriva- tives have *ē* The second pers. sing. of the imperative of the second; but *cave, vide, vale* Monosyllables; but enclitics follow the rule Adverbs from adjectives in "us;" but benĕ, malĕ Fermē, ferē, ohē; *superne,* *inferne* *l* săl, sŏl, nĭl *r* aĕr, æthĕr, cŭr, fār, fŭr, lăr, păr (with its compounds), and nouns in "ēr" in- creasing *long* *is* "is" in all plural cases In nouns which increase *long* In the second pers. sing. of verbs when the second pers. pl. makes "ītis;" as, sīs, nolīs † Forīs, gratīs, vīs *(force)* and vīs *(from* volo) *us* "ŭs" fem. of the third "ūs" of the fourth in all cases but the nom. sing. "ūs" in Monosyllables

§ 13. A *short* final syllable ending in a consonant becomes *long*

* The *o* in the nom. of nouns and in verbs and gerunds is said to be common, but it is very seldom found short.
† The "*is*" sing. in the second future, and the perf. subj. is common.

when it is followed by a word beginning with any *consonant* except *h ;* as, *vincit gloria.*

§ 14. A *short* final syllable ending in a vowel is *sometimes* made *long* when the next word begins with *sc, sp,* or *st,* as *telā scandere.*

§ 15. A final syllable ending in a vowel, whether long or short, *is cut off* when the next word begins with a vowel or *h ;* thus, *intentique ora* becomes *intentiqu' ora.* This is called *Synalœpha.*

§ 16. A final syllable ending in *m* is *cut off* when the next word begins with a vowel or with *h ;* thus, *quanquam animus* becomes *quanqu' animus.* This is called *Ecthlipsis.*

§ 17. To *Scan* a verse is to divide it into the feet of which it is composed ; marking the quantity of each syllable.

§ 18. This is best done by marking, 1. the quantity of the syllables which may be known from the general rules ; 2. of the final syllables, paying attention to the rules in § 13—16 ; and, 3. in a hexameter, of the dactyl and spondee at the end. The vacancies may then be easily filled up, especially by bearing in mind that a *short* syllable must *always* be preceded or followed by *another short* syllable.

Ex. Tūnc mĭhĭ | vītă fŏ | rēt dūl | cĭs, nēc | trĭs tĭă | nōssēm.

　　Bēllă, nĕc | aūdĭs | sēm ‖ cōrdĕ mĭ | cāntĕ tŭ | băm.

Here, in the hexameter, all the syllables may be marked from the rules, except *hi, vi,* and *fo.* Now "*hi*" must be short to *complete the dactyl;* "*vi*" must be long to *begin the next foot;* and "*fo*" must be short for the same reason as "*hi.*" In the pentameter all may be marked except *mi* and *tu,* and the quantity of each of these is then obvious.

By this means only can we learn the quantity of a vowel before *one* consonant.